your Li!

CLAIMED FOR
THE DESERT
PRINCE'S HEIR

CLAIMED FOR THE DESERT PRINCE'S HEIR

HEIDI RICE

MILLS & BOON

First published in Great Britain 2019
by Mills & Boon, an imprint of HarperCollins*Publishers*
1 London Bridge Street, London, SE1 9GF

Large Print edition 2020

© 2019 Heidi Rice

ISBN: 978-0-263-08449-8

MIX
Paper from
responsible sources
FSC™ C007454

This book is produced from independently certified
FSC™ paper to ensure responsible forest management. For
more information visit www.harpercollins.co.uk/green.

Printed and bound in Great Britain
by CPI Group (UK) Ltd, Croydon, CR0 4YY

To Daisy.
Thanks for the fabulous brainstorming
session that turned Raif from a
desert rogue into a Modern hero!
Mwah! xx

CHAPTER ONE

KASIA SALAH SQUINTED at the heat haze on the horizon and the ominous cloud of dust that shimmered above it, then glared at her mobile phone.

No service.

She breathed the swear word she'd learned during her years at Cambridge University as sweat collected on her upper lip and trickled down her back beneath her T-shirt and the voluminous robe she wore to stave off the heat and dust of the desert landscape. It was the sort of swear word she would have been punished by her grandmother for even knowing—let alone saying—once upon a time. She tucked her smartphone into the back pocket of her shorts, taking several more frustrating moments to locate it under the miles of fabric. Then transferred her glare to the engine of the black SUV—and swore again, louder this time. After all, there was no one within a fifty-mile radius to hear her—and it felt empowering, even if it wasn't going to help.

Why hadn't she thought to take a satellite phone with her before leaving the palace for this research trip? Or a companion? Preferably one who knew a bit more than she did about car mechanics? She sighed and kicked the tyre of the broken-down Jeep.

It had been reckless, over-confident and overly optimistic...her three favourite flaws.

Then again, she hadn't intended to break down in the middle of nowhere with no phone signal.

Sheikh Zane Ali Nawari Khan, her best friend Catherine's husband, the ruler of Narabia and, nominally, her boss, had worked long and hard to bring internet connectivity and a cellphone network to large parts of the kingdom. But she suspected she was too close to the borderlands here—an undeveloped desert, flanked by the mountain region in the south, populated only by the Kholadi nomads. From what she could remember, the Kholadi didn't even have running water, so the chances of them needing a phone signal were fairly slim.

Using the robe to cover her hands, so she didn't burn them on the hot metal, she unhooked the defunct vehicle's bonnet. It slammed down, the sound echoing in the febrile air. Luckily, she had given Cat and her assistant Nadia a detailed itinerary of her day trip, so when she didn't return this evening they would send out a search party.

But that still meant spending a night in the Jeep.

Wasn't that going to be fun, especially when the temperature plummeted as soon as the sun dipped below the desert floor.

The hot, dry wind swept a sprinkle of sand into her face. Tugging the robe's head scarf over her nose and mouth so she didn't inhale the gritty swirls, she peered towards the horizon. The cloud she had spotted earlier had grown, spreading across the land in both directions and blotting out the shimmering heat haze like a malevolent force.

Adrenaline kicked at her ribs like one of Zane's thoroughbred Arabian stallions. And the anxiety she'd been keeping a tight rein on rippled down her spine.

Was that a sandstorm?

And was it headed her way?

She'd never experienced one before, having been cloistered in the luxurious safety of the Golden Palace's women's quarters for most of her life.

But she'd heard about the sandstorms. The carnage they wrought could strike terror into the hearts of grown men and women. Her grandmother had whispered about them in hushed reverential tones; how the worst of them had laid waste to the kingdom, turning farmland back into desert and causing numerous fatalities.

She swallowed down the panic threatening to overwhelm her.

Stop being a drama queen.

It was another one of her flaws. Seeing everything too vividly.

Her grandmother, for all her innate wisdom, had been a drama queen, too. Kasia had been only four years old when she'd gone to live with her, eventually becoming part of the palace staff herself when the old Sheikh had died, and the new Sheikh, Zane, had hired Catherine Smith, a Cambridge scholar, to write a book on the kingdom.

Getting a job as Catherine's personal assistant at the age of nineteen had changed her life— especially when Cat had married Zane and become Narabia's Queen, opening Kasia's eyes to an exciting world beyond the palace walls. She wasn't that over-eager, over-imaginative and overly romantic teenager any more—hiding all her insecurities behind a veil of unfulfillable dreams. She was a grown woman now with dreams she was already achieving of becoming an environmental scientist who would save Narabia's agricultural land from the desert that threatened to consume it.

Some sand and a night in a Jeep wasn't going to faze her...much. In fact, a night spent in the desert might afford her some useful research data.

And who said this was even a sandstorm? There had been no reports of any adverse weather, because she'd checked both the local and the satellite reports before she'd left the palace. She might be reckless, but she was not an idiot.

She repeated the reassuring words, but her gaze remained superglued to the horizon.

The dark, impenetrable cloud grew, blocking out the sun. It had to be at least thirty or forty miles wide, and although it was still a mile away it was advancing fast. The noise cut through the desert silence. Tiny creatures—a lizard, a snake, a rodent—scurried and slithered past her boots, rushing to burrow into the ground. The bright, cloudless sky darkened.

Fear clawed at her throat as her mind tried to engage. Should she get into the SUV? Should she get under it?

Then she saw something—a blot on the horizon—emerge from the cloud like a bullet. It took a while for the shimmering blot to solidify into a silhouette. It was a person, on a horse, galloping fast.

Panic and anxiety tightened around her throat.

Black flowing robes lifted in the wind behind the charging figure, like the wings of a giant predatory bird, as the horse's hooves became audible over the roar of the sand.

The rider was a man. A very big man. His outline broad and strong, the fluid graceful movements powerful and overwhelming as he seemed to become one with the stallion as it galloped at full speed. He wore a headdress, masking most of his face.

The panic wrapped around her heart, the thundering beat matching the clump-clump-clump of the approaching hooves—as she saw the horse and rider change course and veer straight towards her.

Then she noticed the rifle strap crossing his broad chest.

A bandit. What else could he be, miles from civilisation?

Run, Kasia, run.

The silent scream echoed inside her head. The howling winds lifted the sand around her. Then in her grandmother's voice—a voice she had always associated with salvation—*Stay calm. Don't panic. He's just a man.*

But even as she tried to rationalise the fear, liberate herself from the panic—reminding her of the sight of her mother walking away for the last time—a strange melting sensation at her core plunged into her abdomen.

A shout rang out, muffled by his scarf, in a dialect she didn't recognise.

He was almost upon her.

For goodness' sake, Kasia, stop standing there like a ninny and move.

The call to action helped drown out the fear of being alone and defenceless, a fear she had spent years conquering in childhood.

You're not that little girl who wasn't good enough. You're brave and smart and accomplished.

She scrambled round the Jeep, wrenched open the passenger door, and dived into the stuffy interior. The sand peppering the windows sounded like rifle shots as her hand landed on the pistol in the passenger seat.

Zane had insisted she learn to shoot before he would allow her to go into the desert alone. But as her fingers closed over the metal, her heart butted her tonsils.

She knew how to shoot at a target with some degree of accuracy, but she had never shot a living thing.

The charging horse came to an abrupt stop only inches from the SUV's bumper. Scrambling out, the sand slicing her cheeks like a whip, Kasia lifted the pistol in both hands and pressed a trembling finger to the trigger.

'Stop there or I'll shoot,' she shouted in English, because it had become her first language after five years in the UK.

Chocolate eyes narrowed above the mask—glittering with intent and fury. The warmth in her abdomen became hot and heavy. And all the more terrifying.

The bandit swung a leg over the horse's neck and jumped down in one fluid movement without speaking, those dark eyes burning into her soul.

She jerked back a step and the pistol went off.

The pop was barely audible in the storm, but the recoil threw her down hard on her backside and she saw the man jerk back.

Had she hit him?

Before the thought had a chance to register, the stallion reared, its hooves pawing the air above her head. The bandit caught the horse's reins before the animal could trample her into the desert floor, and she felt a rush of relief. Within seconds, though, he loomed over her again and the relief that she hadn't killed him turned to panic. She scrambled back on her bottom, kicked out with her feet.

'Get away from me.'

Where was the gun?

She searched for it frantically, but her vision was all but obscured by the swirling sands. He had become the only focus, the ominous outline bearing down on her.

Long fingers shot from the storm and gripped her arm. He hauled her up, bent down and hefted her onto his shoulder with such speed and strength she could barely grasp what was happening before she found herself straddling the huge black horse's sweat-soaked back.

She lifted her leg, trying to dismount, but before she could get her knee over the pommel, he had mounted behind her.

He grasped the reins with one hand and banded his other arm around her midriff, pulling her into the unyielding strength of his body.

She let out an 'Oomph…' as the air was expelled from her lungs. The iron band of his forearm pressed into her breasts. Then suddenly they were flying, her bottom bouncing on the saddle—abandoning the Jeep, which was already half-buried in sand. Her body was forced to succumb to the will of his much bigger, much stronger one as he bent forward, his robes shielding her from the sand stinging her eyes. She tried to cry out, to fight the lethargy wrought by terror, the visceral heat coursing through her body making her too aware of every place their bodies touched.

He's kidnapping you. You must fight. You must survive.

The words screamed in her head, but her breathing was so rapid now it was painful, her whole body confined, subdued, overwhelmed by his and the storm of sand and dust and darkness raging around them.

They seemed to ride for ever through the swirl

of sand—until eventually her fear and panic stopped crushing her ribs and her body melted into exhaustion. The rhythm of the horse's movements seeped into her bones, the man's unyielding strength cocooning her against the elements.

Was this Stockholm syndrome? she wondered vaguely, her tired mind no longer capable of engaging with the terror as her body succumbed to the impenetrable darkness, the controlled purpose of her captor's movements and the stultifying heat coursing through her.

As her eyes drifted shut and her bones turned to water, she dropped down through the years, until she became that little girl again. But this time she was no longer alone and defenceless, her mother gone without a backward glance, but sheltered in strong arms against the storm.

CHAPTER TWO

KASIA WOKE AGAIN in fits and starts. First the bristle of cold on her face, and the heavy weight at her back, both suffocating and warming her. As Kasia opened her eyes, her heart swelled into her throat.

Red light glowed on the horizon, starlight was sprinkled overhead. Shooting stars shot across the sky, illuminating the desert dunes. Her thighs trembled and she became aware of the large warm bulk between them.

A horse. She was on a horse.

His horse.

Memory flooded back.

Kidnapped!

She'd been kidnapped by the man whose muscular forearm banded around her waist. And whose body radiated heat as it cocooned hers.

All the inappropriate dreams she'd had about him returned, too. She shoved them to one side and tried to free her arms.

You're not in Stockholm any more!

A grunt sounded next to her ear, making her aware of the unearthly quiet of the night, the chill of the evening breeze. The storm had passed.

And she was alone, in the middle of the desert, with the bandit who had captured her. And saved her. But why?

Whatever. Now it was time to save herself. From him.

The horse's hooves thudded patiently against the rocky dunes as they rose over a hill. An oasis came into view in the valley below. The horse picked its way down the slope as sure-footed as a cat. The mirrored expanse of water reflected the dying red of the sunset, palm trees and plants grew in profusion around the water's edge. The rasp of her kidnapper's breathing echoed in her ears, making her heart thunder against her ribs.

Was that arousal she could hear in his rough breathing? How would she know? She'd never been in a man's arms before when he was aroused.

Not the point, Kasia. Focus. For goodness' sake.

The numbness in her fingers as she gripped the saddle horn tingled, her thighs quivered and burned, sore from what had to have been several hours on horseback. She became aware of the stinging pain where the sandstorm had abraded her exposed skin and got into her eyes.

She gulped, trying to force her tired mind to come up with a plan.

If he'd saved her from the storm, maybe he wasn't planning to hurt her, now would be a good time to start talking to him.

'Thank you for saving me from the sandstorm,' she said, with as much authority as she could muster with her throat raw and her body brutally aware of the solid chest imprinted on her back. 'I'm a close friend of the Queen. She will pay you handsomely for returning me to the palace now.' The words flowed out, sounding impossibly loud in the quiet night.

But he didn't reply, his body pressing heavily against her as the horse approached the water. She spotted a large tent erected in a copse of palm trees. The horse loped to a stop in front of the tent, and her heartbeat careered into her throat.

The scent of fresh water dispelled the fetid odour of horse and the salty scent of the man.

She pushed his chest with her shoulder, freeing her arms from their confinement.

He grunted again, the sound trailing off into a moan, but strangely the panic from earlier didn't return.

He was big and clearly very strong, having ridden for miles to escape the storm, but the way he was holding her didn't feel threatening. It felt protective.

Unless that was just her cockeyed optimism taking another trip to Stockholm.

But he'd made no move to hurt her. So she clung onto her optimism—cockeyed or not—and repeated her promise of riches again in Narabian, but still got no response.

They sat together on the horse in silence, her whole body brutally aware of each subtle shift in his.

She could feel the thigh muscles that cupped her hips flex, sending a shaft of something hot and fluid through her. The wave of arousal shocked her. How could she be turned on? When she didn't even know if this man was a good guy or not?

He shifted again, his moan shivering down her

spine. But then the arm around her waist loosened. And his body began to slide to one side.

What the...? Was he dismounting?

She squeezed the horse's sides with her knees and grasped the saddle horn. The rush of air at her back as his hot weight slid away was followed by a loud thud.

She gazed down to see the man lying on the ground beneath the horse.

'Whoa, boy,' she whispered frantically, scared the horse might bolt. But after stamping its hooves far too close to the man's head, it settled, its tail swishing.

How could he have fallen off the horse? Was he asleep? Was that why he hadn't replied? He had to be even more exhausted than she was after their ride.

The questions whipped around her brain. Relief and confusion tangled in her belly.

Leaning over the horse's neck, she grasped the dangling reins. She hadn't ridden a horse since leaving Narabia for the UK, and certainly never one this enormous, but as she went to kick the horse with her heels, she glanced down at the man again. He hadn't moved, the lump of his body just lying there on the ground. Her legs relaxed and, instead of spurring the horse on, she found herself scrambling down from the huge beast.

Perhaps she was nuts—a cockeyed optimist with a side order of starry-eyed romantic—but she just couldn't bring herself to ride away and leave him lying there. Not after spending what had to have been several hours sleeping in his arms while he'd ridden them both to safety.

Landing on the other side, she grasped the reins and drew the animal further away from the rider's inert form.

She tried to lead the horse to the tent in the trees, but it wouldn't budge, simply snuffling and lifting its muzzle. 'You don't want to leave him, is that it?'

The horse bounced its head as if it was nodding.

Oh, for... Get a grip, Kasia. Horses don't speak English—especially not Narabian bandit horses.

Eventually she gave up trying to coax the horse away. And stepped closer to the man's prone figure. He hadn't moved, but still she approached him with caution. He'd looked enormous on the horse, and being flat on his back didn't seem to diminish his stature much.

A shooting star lit up the dark sky, and she gasped as bright light exploded above her, shedding its glow over the man at her feet. The black headdress covering his head and his nose and mouth had fallen off. He had wavy, dark hair, which stood up in sweaty tufts, but it was his strikingly handsome face that stole her breath.

The sight was imprinted on her retinas as the light died and the shadows returned. High slashing cheekbones, black brows, and sun-burnished skin pulled tight over the perfect symmetry of his features. He had several days' worth of stubble covering the bottom half of his face, but even with the disguising beard, she'd never seen a man as gorgeous. Even Sheikh Zane couldn't hold a candle to him, his features less refined than the Sheikh's but so much more compelling.

So not the point, Kaz. Who cares if he looks like a movie star? He's still a bandit.

But he was the movie star bandit who had saved her, so there was that.

Gathering every ounce of purpose and determination she possessed, she knelt beside him, close enough to make out his features in the dying light. Why did he look familiar?

Another meteor trailed across the night sky,

illuminating his face. Shock combined with the heat burning low in her belly as recognition struck.

She gasped. 'Prince Kasim?'

Ruler of the Kholadi. He had attended Zane and Cat's wedding five and a half years ago. She knew all the rumours and gossip about this man—that he was the illegitimate son of one of the old Sheikh's concubines, thrown out of the palace as a boy when Zane, the Sheikh's legitimate heir, had been kidnapped from his American mother in LA and brought to Narabia as a teenager. The story went that Kasim had crawled through the desert only to be treated with equal contempt by his mother's nomadic tribe—until he had forced his way to the top of the Kholadi using the fighting skills he'd honed as he'd grown to manhood.

She'd adored all those stories, they'd been so compelling, so dramatic, and had made him seem even more mythic and dangerously exciting, not that she'd needed to put him on any more of a pedestal after setting eyes on him as a nineteen-year-old at Zane and Cat's wedding.

Clothed in black ceremonial wear, he'd strode into the palace at the head of a heavily armed honour guard of Kholadi tribesman, and stolen her breath, like that of every other girl and woman there. He'd been tall and arrogant and magnificent—part warrior, all chieftain, all man—and much younger than she'd expected. He must have been in his mid-twenties at that wedding because he'd only been seventeen when he had become the Kholadi Chief. After years of battling with his own father's army, he had negotiated a truce with Narabia when Zane had come to the throne.

Observing him from afar during the wedding and a few other official visits before she'd left for Cambridge, Kasia had become a little obsessed with the warrior prince. His prowess with women was almost as legendary as his skill in combat and his political agility. She'd adored all the stories that had trickled down into the palace's women's quarters after every visit— about how manly his physique was unclothed, how impressive his 'assets', how he could make a woman climax with a single glance. Like every other piece of gossip in the quarters, those salacious stories had been embellished and enhanced, but every time she'd had a chance to assess his broad, muscular physique or that rakish, devil-may-care smile from afar, she would fantasise that every word was true—and want to be the next woman on whom he bestowed that smile, and so much more.

He'd been a myth to her then, an object of her febrile adolescent desires, who had been larger than life in every respect. But he was just a man now.

The ripple of heat that she had been trying and failing to ignore sank deeper into her sex.

They didn't call him the Bad-Boy Sheikh for nothing.

She stared at him, unable to believe she'd pointed a gun at him. Thank goodness she hadn't actually shot him. Despite his wicked ways, he was a powerful prince. Plus, he'd rescued her. From a sandstorm.

As she pondered that far too romantic thought his eyelids fluttered.

The dark chocolate gaze fixed on her face and the heat in her sex blossomed like a mushroom cloud.

'Prince Kasim, are you okay?' she asked, the question popping out in English. She repeated it in Narabian. Did he even speak English?

He grunted again and she noticed for the first

time the sheen of sweat on his forehead, and that his gaze, so intense earlier, now looked dazed. Then he replied in accented English.

'My name is Raif. Only my brother calls me by my Narabian name.' The husky rasp was expelled on a breath of outrage. 'And, no I'm not okay, you little witch. You shot me.'

The bullet *had* hit him?

'I'm so sorry,' she yelped. But before she could say more, his eyes closed.

The darkness was descending fast, but gripping his robe she tugged it away to reveal bare skin beneath. Scars—so many scars—and a tattoo marred the smooth skin, making the bunch of muscle and sinew look all the more magnificent.

She ignored the well of heat pulsing at her core. *So, so not the point, Kaz.*

She pressed trembling fingers to his chest, felt the muscles tense as she frantically ran them over his ribs up to his shoulder to locate the wound. Her fingertips encountered sticky moisture. She drew her hand away, her eyes widening in horror at the stain of fresh blood. The metallic smell invaded the silent night.

She swore again, the same word that had made her feel empowered several hours ago when she'd found herself alone in the desert with a broken-down Jeep.

Now she was alone in the desert with a bleeding man. A bleeding, unconscious warrior prince, who had saved her from a sandstorm and whom she'd shot for his pains.

She'd never felt less empowered in her life.

CHAPTER THREE

'YOU'RE NOT MY SON—you're not anyone's son. You're nothing more than vermin—a rat, born by mistake.'

The angry memory ripped through Raif's body, his heart pounding so hard it felt as if it would gag him. His father's face reared up, the cruel slant of his lips, the contempt in his flat black eyes, the cold echo of the only words he'd ever spoken to him cutting through the familiar nightmare like a rusting blade.

'I clothed and fed you for ten years. You are a man now—any responsibility I had is paid. Now, get out.'

'No...' The desperate cry came out of his mouth, shaming, pathetic, pleading.

The crack of his father's hand sounded like a rifle shot, although the ache wasn't in his cheekbone this time but his arm. He shifted, trying to escape the cruel words, the bitter memories. The echo of remembered pain, too real and so vivid.

'Shh… Prince Raif, you're having a bad dream. Everything is okay, really, it was just a flesh wound.'

Soft words in English drifted to him through the cloaking agony. Something cool and soft fluttered over his brow. Like the wings of an angel.

'Not a prince…a rat,' he whispered back in the same language.

An exotic fragrance—jasmine, spice and female sweat—floated through the night on a cooling breeze. His nostrils flared like those of a stallion scenting its mate. The warmth of the night settled into his groin, swelling his shaft. He concentrated his mind on the pulse of pleasure, let it flow through him, to dull the aching pain always left by the nightmare in his heart.

Not a rat. You're a prince… And a man now, not an unloved boy.

He thought the words but swallowed them, remembering even through his exhaustion that he should never admit to a weakness. Not to anyone.

Soft fingers touched his chin, then something cold pressed against his lips.

The urgent female voice spoke again but he couldn't hear what it said because of the blood rushing in his ears. And the heat hurtling beneath his belt.

The taste of fresh water invaded his senses. He opened his mouth, gulping as the liquid soothed his dry throat.

'Slow down or you'll choke.' The voice was less gentle, firm, demanding—he liked it even more. But then it took the refreshing water away.

He dragged open his eyelids, which had rocks attached to them.

The pleasure swelled and throbbed in his groin.

'Who are you?' he whispered in Kholadi.

The hazy vision was exquisite, like an angel, or a temptress—flushed skin, wild midnight hair, and large eyes the same colour as precious amber, the shade only made more intense by the bruised shadows under them and the wary glow of embarrassment and knowledge.

I want you.

Had he said that aloud?

'I can't understand you, Prince Raif. I don't speak Kholadi.' The lush lips moved, but the address confused him. Why was she mixing his Narabian title with his tribal name?

'Beautiful,' he whispered in English, his fatigued brain not able to engage with the vagaries of his cultural heritage. He wanted to touch her skin and see if it was as soft as it looked, to capture that pointed chin and bring her mouth down to his, trace the cupid's bow on the top lip with his tongue, but as he lifted his hand, the twinge of pain in his arm made him flinch.

'Lie still and go back to sleep, it's not morning yet, Prince Raif.'

Prince Raif? Who is that? I am not Prince to the Kholadi. I am their Chief.

He gritted his teeth as her cool fingers brushed his chest, an oasis in the midst of the warm night.

'Not an angel…' he said, trying to cling to consciousness, wanting to cling to her, so the nightmare would not return. 'A witch.' Then the sweet, hazy vision faded as the rocks rolled back over his eyes and he plunged back into sleep.

Beautiful.

Kasia stared down at the man she'd been lying beside for several hours now.

Lifting the cloth out of the bowl of warming water beside the bed, she squeezed out the excess liquid with cramping fingers. Placing it on his chest, she brushed it over the contours of muscle and bone shiny with sweat. The now familiar prickle of awareness sped up her arm as she glided the cooling cloth over the taut inked skin of his shoulder.

The red and black serpent tattoo that curled around his collar bone and covered his shoulder blade shimmered in the flicker of light from the kerosene lamps she'd lit as night fell.

She blinked, forcing herself to remain upright and focused. His cheeks above the line of his beard were a little flushed but he didn't have a fever, thank goodness. Surely the rambling that had woken him up had just been a nightmare.

As he sank back into sleep, his breathing deepened.

He'd managed to swallow a fair portion of the water this time.

She re-dipped the cloth and continued to sweep it over the broad expanse of his chest, her gaze drawn to the scars that had made her wince after wrestling him out of his bloodstained robe the night before.

How could one man have sustained so much damage in his life? And survived?

Heat flushed through her as she followed the white puckered mark of an old wound into the sprinkle of masculine hair that tapered into a fine line and arrowed beneath his pants.

Her gaze connected with the prominent ridge pressing against the loose black cloth—the only piece of clothing she hadn't been brave enough to take off him.

Soaked with sweat, his pants didn't leave much to her imagination as they clung to the long muscles of his flanks and outlined the huge ridge she'd noticed several times during the last few hours.

A sight that managed to both relieve and disturb her in equal measure. Surely he couldn't be badly hurt if he could sport such an impressive erection? But what kind of man could be aroused after getting shot, however superficial the wound had turned out to be?

Look away from the erection. Maybe it's a natural state for a man suffering from exhaustion? How would you know? You've never slept with a man before, and you've certainly never shot one.

The blush burned as she dipped the cloth once more and concentrated on wiping the new film of sweat from his skin. And not getting absorbed again in his aroused state.

She ought to be used to that mammoth erection by now. After all she'd spent rather a lot of time trying to gauge its size.

Seriously? Look away! And stop objectifying a stranger.

She forced her wayward gaze back to his upper torso.

The bandage she'd applied several hours ago remained unstained.

Thank goodness the bullet had only grazed his upper arm. Her first-aid skills did not extend to conducting emergency surgery in a tent. She'd lost her own phone when he'd rescued her. And she hadn't been able to find anything resembling a satellite phone or communication equipment in the tent.

Although tent was far too ordinary a word for the lavish construction where they had been co-cooned since nightfall.

She glanced around the structure, astonished all over again by the luxurious interior she'd discovered after managing to rouse her patient to get him off the desert floor and into his dwelling.

A dwelling more than fit for a desert prince.

Rich silks covered the walls of the chamber that held the large bed pallet and an impressive array of hunting equipment, chests full of tinned and dried goods, clothing and even a battery-powered icebox packed with meat and perishable food. Thankfully she had also discovered medical supplies, which she'd used to clean and bandage his wound. She had even found a goat tethered at the back of the encampment where there was a corral and a shelter for his horse and a smaller pack pony.

How long had Prince Raif, or Prince Kasim, as she had always heard him addressed before he had corrected her, been living here, and why was he living here alone? Or was this simply an emergency shelter the Kholadi kept stocked for tribespeople caught alone in the desert?

Stop asking questions you can't answer.

She dumped the cloth in the bowl and sat on her haunches, a wave of exhaustion making her feel light-headed.

She examined her patient, and pressed the back of her hand to his brow. She released a breath. Still normal, no sign of any adverse effects from his wound.

After several hours of getting intimately acquainted with this man's face and body, hearing the strange plea she couldn't understand in his nightmares, she had no desire to hurt him more than she already had.

The guilt had crippled her at first. But as the minutes had stretched into hours, her vigil had morphed into something strangely cathartic.

Prince Raif fascinated her, he always had even from afar. But he fascinated her even more now, bandaged and virtually naked, flushed with what she suspected was a mild case of heatstroke from their exhausting escape and with the evidence of his own mortality—and the harsh reality of his life—visible in those scars and that striking tattoo. Awareness prickled and glowed, making her skin tighten over her bones and her heart thump against her ribs.

The crack of a log in the fire outside the tent made her jump. She shook her head, trying to dispel the fugue state into which she seemed to be descending.

He'd called her a witch and—while he had a valid reason to think she was one, after all she *had* shot him—she'd also seen hunger in his eyes. A hunger that had disturbed her as much as it had excited her.

The visceral intimacy that had been created by his rescue and her recent vigil was an illusion.

Prince Raif was famous, or rather infamous, for seducing any woman he wanted and then discarding her.

Another crackle from the fire forced her tired mind to unlock.

Getting a bit ahead of yourself there, Kaz.

Worrying about how she was going to explain shooting him when he woke up made more sense than worrying about how she was going to resist a seduction that hadn't happened.

She forced her gaze away from his mesmerising body and out towards the desert. The shimmer of light on the horizon as dawn began to seep over the dunes was gilded by the orange and gold flames leaping from the fire pit.

The desert was another world, wild and beautiful and sophisticated in its own way—especially its eco-system. But it was a world she had never been a part of, cocooned as she had been in the Sheikh's palace and then the world of UK academia.

She had never known a man like Prince Raif, however well she might once have wanted to know him, or how well she now knew the contours of his harsh body, the design of his tattoo.

Forcing herself to her feet, she stumbled out

of the tent, absorbed the glorious beauty of another desert sunrise, then walked to the corral, watered the horse and brought back an armful of wood. She fed the fire, aware the temperature would remain low until the sun rose fairly high in the sky.

As she staggered back into the tent her gaze tracked inexorably to the Prince's broad chest. She watched it rise and fall in a regular rhythm, the nightmares no longer tormenting him. The serpent tattoo coiled around his shoulder in the flicker of lamplight—as vibrant as the man it adorned.

Her heart lifted and swelled with relief. He would be fine. She hadn't hurt him too badly.

He looked peaceful now—or as peaceful as a man as large and powerful as he was could ever look.

She lay down, curled up beside him and dragged the soft blanket over the T-shirt and shorts ensemble she'd been living in for nearly twenty-four hours as the night's chill seeped into her weary bones.

She needed sleep. And however frivolous or foolishly romantic the urge, she wanted to stay beside him, just in case he had another of those nasty nightmares.

She placed her hand over his heart. She absorbed the steady rhythm and the sharp tug of awareness. She could feel the puckered skin of an old wound. Okay, maybe she didn't want to lie beside him just for the sake of his health or well-being. But what harm could it do?

She'd never get another opportunity to touch him like this, and maybe she owed this much to the fanciful girl she'd been, the girl she'd thought had died during all those hours of reading and studying, a world away. She was glad that girl hadn't died completely, because she'd always liked her.

'Sleep well, Prince Raif,' she whispered.

As soon as her lids closed, she dropped into the deep well that had been beckoning her for hours. Vivid erotic dreams leapt and danced like the flames in the fire pit and the shooting stars in the desert night, full of heat and purpose, both dazzling and intoxicating.

But the dreams didn't disturb her any more, because with them came the fierce tug of yearning.

CHAPTER FOUR

RAIF JERKED AWAKE, then slammed his eyes shut again as the light from the sun shining into the tent seemed to burn his retinas.

Why was he lying in bed at midday?

But as soon as he shifted, he felt the twinge in his arm, and he knew. The memories assailed him all at once. The deafening sound of the storm, the pop of gunfire, the sharp recoil as a bullet glanced off his flesh. The scent of jasmine and sweat during the endless ride to safety, the long night of exhausted sleep and nightmares, the sound of voices—his father's sneering contempt from many years ago and the pleas of an angel to lie still, to drink, not to drink too fast…

She'd been quite a bossy angel now he thought about it.

Not an angel, a witch. She'd tried to shoot him—the fierce look in her eyes as she'd pointed the pistol at him both arousing and infuriating. A rueful smile edged his mouth, but then he hissed as his dry lips cracked.

He closed his eyes and became one with his body—a process he'd learned as a boy through brutal experience—to assess his injuries.

His arm was a little stiff, but not as stiff as when he'd been kicked by his stallion Zarak a week ago on his first trip back to the tribal lands in over five months.

The gap had been too long since his last return, and the stallion—always high-spirited—had thrown a temper tantrum.

Zarak had missed him, but not as much as he'd missed Zarak, and the landscape, the culture, the people who had saved him as a child—and turned him into a man.

But this trip had been fraught with surprises. After leaving the desert encampment, in the outskirts of the tribal lands, to spend time alone at his private oasis, to enjoy the challenge of being a man again—instead of a chieftain, or a prince, or a business tycoon—the sandstorm had struck.

He moved his arm, testing its limits. The mild ache that had woken him during the night was gone now. Unlike the more pressing ache in his groin.

A gust of breath raised the hair on his chest and made the pounding in his groin intensify. He blinked, letting his eyes adjust to the light, and turned, to see the vision he had encountered the night before.

It was her. The angel. The witch.

She lay beside him, fast asleep. Her wild hair, tied in a haphazard ponytail, accentuated her exquisite beauty—high cheekbones, kissable lips, and those large eyes, closed now as she lay sleeping.

How old was she? Early twenties? Definitely more a woman than a girl. Bold enough to aim a gun at him.

And where was she from? The dust-stained T-shirt stretched enticingly over her breasts bore the insignia of the same British university Catherine, the Queen of Narabia, had attended. With her colouring, the girl could be a native of this part of the world, but she was dressed like a student in LA or London.

The swell of arousal grew as he examined the toned thighs displayed by her shorts.

The colour in her cheeks heightened and her breathing became irregular. Her eyelids flickered, the rapid eye movements suggesting she was having a vivid dream. Could she sense him observing her?

He had to stifle a smile when she moaned—the sound so husky it seemed to stroke his erection. Was she dreaming about him? He hoped so, because he had dreamed of her.

She mumbled something in her sleep, shifted and then her small hand, which had been resting on the bedding, reached out to touch his chest. He gritted his teeth as her fingertips slid over his nipple and down his ribs, trailing fire in their wake, and turning his erection to iron, before getting tantalisingly close to the waistband of his pants. Her touch dropped away abruptly as she rolled over—giving him a nice view of her pert bottom.

He wetted his lips, struggling to quell the brutal pulse of unrequited desire and ignore the stab of something else at the loss of her touch.

Disappointment? Regret? Longing?

He remembered the same feeling from the night before when he'd had the recurring nightmare, and he'd clung to her compassion. Which was not like him. He didn't need tenderness from anyone.

He'd been alone all his life, had been shot at

many times and had survived much worse than a sandstorm. He had made it his mission never to rely on the kindness of others. If his life had taught him one thing—both as a boy in the desert and as a man in the boardrooms of Manhattan—it was that no one could be trusted. That life was brutal and survival was all that counted. That weakness would destroy you.

Dragging his gaze away from the girl's perfectly rounded backside, he sat up. Taking a deep breath, he got a lungful of his own scent.

Damn, he smelt worse than Zarak after a day-long ride. His stomach growled so loudly he was surprised he didn't wake the girl. He must eat and wash. And tend to Zarak, and the goat and the pack pony. He could decide what to do with the woman later. If she came from the Golden Palace, the seat of his brother Zane's power in the neighbouring kingdom of Narabia, he supposed he would have to return her at some point.

He tugged off the blanket covering his lap, then risked another rueful smile at the evidence of his arousal.

He'd been forced to rescue the woman when he'd spotted her stranded by her Jeep. But maybe having her here didn't have to be bad. These few days alone were supposed to be an escape from the burden of leadership, a chance to reconnect with the basics of his life before he had become Kholadi Chief well over a decade ago at the age of seventeen.

His role as Chief had become a great deal more complex and challenging five years ago, when the decision to mine the huge deposits of minerals had given his people vast riches. Riches that had to be managed and invested to give his tribe a more settled, secure existence. It had been his mission to use the wealth to alleviate the hardships of life in the desert and give the tribe's younger generation choices he had lacked. But dragging the Kholadi into the twenty-first century, while protecting the traditions that had shaped their lives for generations, was a juggling act, which had only become more difficult as his life abroad had dragged him away from the homeland that had defined and sustained him.

What better way to relax and escape those burdens than to lose himself in a woman, if she were willing? How long was it since he'd had the chance to enjoy such soft fragrant flesh, to explore the pleasures of an angel? Or a witch?

He rose to his feet, and made his way out of

the tent. As he breathed in the dry desert air, and the sun burnished his skin, his usual vitality returned.

Once he had washed and eaten, he would wake the girl. And see if she was as open as he was to some harmless fun before he returned her to the palace.

Kasia woke slowly, then shot up so fast she had to breathe through the dizziness.

Where was the Prince?

The bed beside her was empty. Bright sunlight shone through the open flaps of the enormous tent.

She scrambled out of the bedding and raced to the entrance. Had he left her here? Gone for a stroll? How long had she slept?

Guilt assailed her all over again as she recalled bandaging the cut on his arm, listening to the rambling cries of his nightmare, and paying far too much attention to the impressive ridge in his pants.

She shielded her eyes against the bright sunlight, blinking furiously as she headed to the corral to search for her rescuer.

The stallion's head lifted and it whinnied, before returning its muzzle to the trough full of fresh water. At least he hadn't ridden away in disgust.

The sound of the spring water tumbling over the red rocks of the oasis beckoned. After giving the stallion's nose a pat, she edged through the grove of palm trees towards the blue pool created in the rock crevice.

She spotted the bandage first, lying unravelled on the ground, the flecks of dried blood making her stomach hurt. Then the black pants, hooked over a desert shrub. Standing at the edge of the trees, her bare feet sinking into the wet sand by the water's edge, she scanned the pool.

Heat raged to every one of her erogenous zones as she spotted her patient, standing under the waterfall.

Her nipples tightened, and her thighs weakened, the moisture pooling in her pants like the water gushing from the rock face.

Wow!

Thigh deep in water and with his back to her, Prince Raif was every teenage fantasy she'd ever had made flesh. All strong lines and hard contours, the serpent tattoo coiling over his shoulder, the bruising from the cut on his arm just one of the many scars marring the smooth brown skin. Her gaze dropped to the tight orbs of his backside, which flexed as he scrubbed the water through thick dark hair.

Goodness, he was even more magnificent naked than he had been in full ceremonial wear at Zane and Cat's wedding.

Kasia stood transfixed, knowing she should move, to leave him to bathe in peace. Hadn't she already caused him enough trouble?

But instead she watched him, absorbing the beauty of his hard male body. She'd never seen a naked man before. Not one in the full prime of manhood. She'd been asked on dates during her years in Cambridge, but had always shied away from making any kind of commitment outside her studies. She hadn't partied much because she'd wanted to return to Narabia with an education that would make her an asset to Narabia's ongoing struggle to become self-sufficient.

Cat and Zane had invested a fortune in her education. Cat had always insisted the money was not important, that Kasia had earned the opportunity after her years at the palace. But she wanted to be worthy of that investment. She was the first native Narabian woman to get such an opportunity. And she intended to be the first of many. Her studiousness had never felt a burden, though, until this moment.

She had no experience of what to do with a physical attraction so intense it scared her a little.

She'd always been curious about sex and excited to explore it—when the time was right. But as she watched the Prince's butt muscles bunch and flex as he bent to scoop more water over his head, her breath clogged in her lungs and she wondered if it was possible to be too aroused. Too excited. Because the tightness in her nipples, the looseness in her thighs, and the gush of longing in her panties was becoming painful. And her heartbeat was so frantic she was concerned she might pass out.

She breathed, trying to ease the sensations besieging her body, but then the Prince turned and began to wade towards her.

Her gaze devoured his full-frontal male glory. *Oh, my...*

Her thundering heartbeat crashed into her throat.

His chest was as broad and heavily muscled as it had appeared last night, but now his skin glowed with health and vitality. He had his head bent, to watch his step as he strode over the rocks in the pool, giving her precious seconds to absorb every inch of him unobserved.

And there were a lot of inches.

He had to be at least a foot taller than her. But as her thirsty gaze drank in the sight of mile-wide shoulders and the washboard ridges of his abdominal muscles, it was drawn downwards.

Even no longer erect, his penis did not disappoint, completing the mesmerising picture of strong, sensual masculinity.

She blinked, suddenly aware he was no longer moving.

She jerked her gaze to his face. Flaming heat blasted across her chest, flooded up her neck and exploded in her cheeks.

'Good afternoon, little witch,' he said, in perfect English—his deep chocolate gaze sparkling with mocking humour. 'Are you assessing the damage?'

'I...' The word came out on a squeak. She swallowed, folding her arms over her chest to control the ache in her nipples. It didn't help.

'I'm so sorry I shot you, Prince Raif.'

And I've just invaded your privacy by ogling you naked while you bathe.

She kept the last part of her apology to herself. He didn't seem bothered that she was seeing him naked. Arrogance and confidence issued from every perfect pore.

'Prince...*who*?' His lips quirked. Even with the beard covering the lower half of his face, the half-smile was devastating. '*What* did you call me?'

'Prince Raif,' she said, confused. Had she addressed him incorrectly? Wasn't that what he'd told her to call him?

From his amusement it was obvious she'd misunderstood. Perhaps she was supposed to kneel? As she once had before Zane, because he was a sheikh?

But as the man before her strolled the rest of the way out of the pool and stopped in front of her, she resisted the urge to drop to her knees.

He didn't seem particularly outraged by the breach of etiquette. And, anyway, if she knelt down she would be at eye level with his... She jerked her chin up.

Do not stare at his junk again. Haven't you been disrespectful enough already?

'Just Raif,' he corrected her. 'I am not a prince in Kholadi, only Chief.'

There was no *only* about it, she decided as he

reached past her, his pectoral muscles rippling as he snagged the black pants off the shrub where he'd dumped them.

She inhaled the aroma of desert thyme alongside the salty aroma of his skin, gilded now by the sheen of fresh water instead of sweat. He used the cotton to mop the moisture drying on his magnificent chest and swept it through his hair, before finally putting the pants back on.

Her breath released, the muscles of her neck finally allowed to relax as he drew the loose pants up to his waist.

'My brother insisted on giving me the title of Prince Kasim when we reached an accord ten years ago,' he said, bending his head to tie the drawstring. 'But it means nothing in the desert.'

The comment sounded casual, but she detected the edge in his voice.

She knew the Kholadi and the Narabian kingdom had been at war for several years, before the old Sheikh, Tariq, had been incapacitated by a stroke. As soon as Zane had taken control of the throne, he had negotiated a truce with his half-brother and the two countries had lived in harmony ever since.

But it seemed their fraternal relationship

wasn't entirely comfortable. Her heart stalled as she thought of the scars all over his body, and the nightmares that had chased him the night before. Like everyone else, she'd heard the stories of how he had been kicked out of the palace as a boy to make way for his legitimate brother, and left to die in the desert.

She had no idea how much of the myth was true. And she'd never given a lot of thought to the devastating effect a trauma like that might have, because the legend of Prince Kasim's survival and battles to lead the Kholadi had been just that, a legend. A fairy-tale. A myth.

But the myth now seemed as real and raw as this man's scars. Of course, his relationship with his brother would be strained, after being rejected so cruelly by their father.

He might seem strong and invincible, but he could be hurt, just like anyone else.

The wave of compassion washed over her as she took in the torn flesh on his upper arm from the injury she'd caused.

'I should re-bandage your arm,' she said, the guilt choking her. But as she went to touch him, his hand shot out and he grabbed her wrist.

'There is no need,' he said.

'But what if it starts to bleed again?' she said, tears of shame stinging her eyes.

Could he feel her pulse pummelling her wrist in staccato punches? Did he know how aroused she was? Even though he was hurt? And she was the one responsible?

The half-smile returned and spread across his impossibly handsome features, and her pulse sped into overdrive.

He knows.

'It is barely a scratch,' he said, releasing her. 'I have survived much worse.'

'Not from me,' she said, appalled at the thought of all the other scars on his body. Was injury a regular occurrence for him? 'I feel awful that I shot you.'

'You did not shoot me, you missed. And you were scared. You were defending yourself. It is a natural reaction.'

'No, it's not,' she said. 'I've never shot at *any-one* before.' He appeared unmoved.

Because he must live in another world. A harsh, cruel world where people shoot first and ask questions later.

'Would you let me check the wound at least, Prince Kasim?' she said, trying to maintain at least a semblance of decorum. Although decorum was the last thing she felt. 'It would make me feel better.'

He stroked a thumb down the side of her face. 'You can check the wound if you wish, but only if you agree to call me Raif.' His hand dropped away, leaving a trail of goosebumps ricocheting down to her core. 'Given how much of me you have already seen, there is little point in standing on ceremony.'

She shook her head, mesmerised by the husky tenor of his voice and the effect it was having on her.

It was only five minutes later, as he sat on the edge of his bed and she knelt beside him to bandage the wound again, that she realised her error.

Because the memory of his body, wet and naked, only made being with him in his bedchamber, inhaling the intoxicating scent of man and desert, all the more overwhelming.

So much so, she wasn't even sure this was reality any more, because it felt like all her teenage fantasies come to vibrant, vivid life.

'What is your name?' Raif asked, needing a distraction as the girl's fingertips brushed his biceps while she wound the new—and entirely unnecessary—bandage around his arm.

She'd been tending him for two minutes—and controlling the surge of heat to his groin each time she touched him had become excruciating.

Did she know the effect she was having on him? Surely she must.

'Kasia. Kasia Salah,' she said, concentrating on the bandaging. But he noted the bloom of colour darkening her cheeks.

'You are Narabian?' Why did that seem important? He'd slept with women of many different nationalities. He didn't judge women by their geography but by how much he wanted them. And he wanted this woman, very much.

'Yes, I was brought up in the Golden Palace. My grandmother worked there as a cook. I was one of the domestic staff.'

Something unlocked inside his chest. So she was of humble birth. Not unlike him.

'Until I became Cat's assistant,' she added, the hint of pride unmistakeable.

'Cat? Who is Cat?'

'Catherine Smith, who is now Queen Catherine Ali Nawari Khan—you know, the Sheikh's wife,' she said, her chest puffing up. 'She is my best friend. It is because of her I have spent the last five years studying abroad.'

'Not because of yourself?' he asked, annoyed by her willingness to give someone else the credit for her achievements.

Zane's wife was beautiful and accomplished. But no more so than this woman. The only difference was that Catherine Khan hadn't had to fight for her education, the way he would guess Kasia had.

The girl's gaze flashed to his—direct and irritated at his observation.

The heat in his groin surged. Her golden gaze sparkled enticingly when it wasn't shadowed with guilt or shame.

'Well, yes,' she said. 'But… Cat is the reason I sought an education. And she and Zane…' She sank back on her heels, finally having finished caressing his biceps. 'They made it possible for me to study abroad in a place called Cambridge University.'

A place called Cambridge University!

Did she think he had never heard of the British institution? What did she take him for? A savage?

His pride bristled—but he bit down on the urge to correct her.

She had been away from her homeland for five years, meaning all she would know of him was that he was the Sheikh's bastard son—a primitive warlord, an unprincipled womaniser.

The rumours had some truth behind them, especially when he'd been a younger man, and he'd been more than happy to foster them because they had always given him a power and mystique he could use to his advantage—in politics, in business and in his bed.

Being the Bad-Boy Sheikh had been an advantage with women, because they loved the allure of the forbidden, the wild.

Why not exploit Kasia's misconceptions about him? He had never been ashamed of that unloved child, who had been strong enough to survive thirst and starvation in the desert, or the angry teenager who had been savage enough to defeat the Kholadi's greatest warriors and become Chief. His past still lived inside him—and defined him in many ways. It always would. Wasn't it to reconnect with those parts of himself that he had returned to the desert?

Adrenaline raced through his bloodstream.

This woman had seen him helpless, something that had made him uneasy. But being the womanising warlord would put the power back in his hands.

She took a tube of antiseptic cream out of the medical box. 'I noticed some scrapes on your back, where you fell off the horse,' she said as she unscrewed the cap. 'Turn around and I'll dab some of this on them.' She held up a finger covered in ointment. 'Before they get infected.'

'Enough.' Raif captured her wrist, satisfied when he felt her pulse pummel his thumb.

'But I should treat the scratches,' she said.

'It's not my back that hurts.' He interrupted her nonsense.

Taking the hint, her gaze dipped to his lap. The blood pounded into his groin. He was as aroused now as he'd been during the depths of his nightmares.

She lifted her head.

Her pupils dilated, obliterating the rich amber of her irises. She was as aroused as him.

'I... I see what you mean,' she stuttered, desire colouring her skin.

'We have had enough foreplay,' he said.

He preferred to be open and honest with

women about his appetites. When it came to sex, he never played games.

'If you want me as much as I want you, we can take this ache away.' He touched her cheek, not able to keep his hands off any longer, the heat rising at the way her breath hitched. 'If you don't, I will escort you back to the palace.' He let his hand drop. He wasn't usually so abrupt with women, but something about her made it hard for him to be subtle about his needs. 'What is your choice?'

CHAPTER FIVE

I CHOOSE YOU.

'I... I...' Kasia stuttered, the heat in her cheeks nothing compared to the liquid tug in her sex.

Prince Kasim's bold offer seemed to be genuine. With no ands, ifs or buts, just like the man himself.

The tug turned into a yank.

Not Prince Kasim... Raif. She corrected herself. Because he was the furthest thing from a prince at the moment. Even a desert prince.

He had no airs or graces, no polite manners, no etiquette. His desire was basic and unashamed, and so much more compelling because of that. His need was arrogantly displayed by the tension in his jaw, the direct gaze and the thick erection.

'I don't know what to say,' she blurted out. Disconcerted by her own driving need.

She'd flirted with men before, even kissed a few. But she'd never been subjected to such a focused assault on her senses by a man like him—who was so bold and unambiguous.

Why did that seem refreshing, and yet disturbing?

'It is a simple question, Kasia.'

Was it simple? Maybe it was to him. Because he had so much more experience. But she could hardly tell him she had never slept with a man before. It felt too revealing.

His lips quirked beneath the beard. 'Let me make it simpler. Do you want me, Kasia? For I dreamed of having you last night.'

The raw declaration tugged at her romantic heart.

He cupped her cheek, and her breath seized, the rasp of his callused skin sending heat spiralling into her tender sex.

His thumb traced her cheekbone, then slid down her neck into the well of her collarbone. The rabbit punches of her pulse echoed in the sweet spot between her thighs.

'I want to make you sob with pleasure.' His thumb circled her breast through her T-shirt and bra. 'To make your nipples ripen and swell beneath my tongue.'

Her nipples squeezed into peaks, as if already

being subjected to the promised caress. She panted, unable to catch her breath under his intense gaze.

He chuckled, the sound arrogant, and so unbelievably hot she felt burned.

'Tell me you want me, Kasia, and we can feed this hunger.'

'Yes.' The word popped out before she could stop it. 'I want you.'

Surely this didn't have to be wrong? They'd survived a sandstorm. They were young and alive. Their worlds might be miles apart, but here and now she wanted to feed the hunger, too. A hunger that had tantalised her all through the night.

She would return to the palace today. Cat and Zane would be frantic with worry—she'd been lost for over twenty-four hours already. She would go back to Cambridge at the end of the month. She had no intention of venturing into the desert alone after this, so she would be unlikely to see him again.

Why couldn't she have this moment? When she wanted him so much? And what better person to initiate her than a man she had idolised? A man who was supposed to be an incredible lover? A man whose 'assets' she'd been assessing most of the night?

He nodded, accepting her surrender as if he had expected no less. Then he grunted something in his own dialect.

She didn't need a translation, though, when his nostrils flared, his gaze becoming so focused her flesh felt scalded.

Standing, he tugged her to her feet. Framing her face in his hands, he positioned her head, then licked the seam of her lips. She opened for him instinctively. The kiss was firm, coaxing. The hunger roared from her core. She had expected him to devour her, but his tongue danced with hers, allowing her to follow his lead in subtle licks.

But as the hunger built, the driving need became more urgent, and the kiss changed, his tongue exploring her mouth and capturing her sighs as he demanded more.

His hands skimmed up her back underneath her T-shirt. The hook of her bra was released. She gripped his shoulders, overwhelmed by sensation as he cupped her breasts, playing with the responsive nipples until she was sobbing into his mouth, the tight peaks yearning for more.

He lifted his head, his eyes dark and unfocused. 'I want you naked, Kasia.'

The gruff request shimmered across her skin, and the ache in her breasts intensified, the hot spot between her thighs throbbing.

She nodded, no longer capable of coherent speech.

Stepping back, he lifted the grubby T-shirt over her head, disposed of the bra.

She folded her arms over her chest, desperately self-conscious.

'No,' he said as he captured her wrists. 'Do not hide, you are so beautiful.'

She felt beautiful as she forced herself to relax, to let him pull her arms gently away from her body. The morning sunlight gilded his chest, making her aware of the bunch of muscle.

The huge erection stood proud under the loose cotton pants and her mouth watered as she imagined seeing him naked and fully erect. But to her surprise, he sank to his knees in front of her. Undoing the buttons on her shorts, he watched her as he drew the denim down with her panties. His rough hands slid down her legs, stripping her bare with exquisite tenderness.

She stepped out of her shorts at his direction,

the need charging through her system as he blew across the triangle of curls, then pressed his face into her sex.

She gripped his shoulders—so broad, so solid—to steady herself as he opened her with his thumbs and licked.

She shuddered, her ragged panting filling the tent as he lapped at the very heart of her. He held her firmly for the shattering exploration. Licking, sucking, discovering the root of her pleasure and ruthlessly exploiting it.

At last he captured the swollen nub of her clitoris and suckled.

The climax broke over her, the waves battering her body. She collapsed over his shoulder, the afterglow like an impenetrable cloud of bliss.

'More,' he grunted, as he stood, lifting her.

Within seconds, she lay on the bed as he stood over her, blocking out the sunlight. He shucked his pants.

Her gaze devoured his nakedness, her tender sex melting at the sight of that massive erection—even larger and harder than she had imagined.

'I need to be inside you,' he said, as he covered her body with his.

'Yes,' she croaked.

She wanted that thick length inside her. Wanted to recapture the glorious oblivion.

Hooking her leg around his waist, to leave her open to him, he angled her hips.

The pinch of pain made her stiffen as he thrust deep. She choked off a cry, struggling to absorb the overwhelming feel of him, lodged so fully inside her.

He swore, every sinew of his body going deadly still. She couldn't read his features, cast into shadow by the dazzling sunlight, but she could feel his shock.

'You were untouched?' he said, the question coming out on a tortured rasp.

'I'm sorry,' she said. 'I should have told you.'

'Yes, but it is too late now,' he said.

She didn't know what he meant. Was he angry with her? But he didn't sound angry, just stunned.

He touched her cheek, cradled her face.

'Am I hurting you?'

It did hurt a little, he was so large and hard inside her. But she didn't want to lose the connection.

'No,' she said. 'I want to feel the pleasure again.'

He buried his face into her neck, pressed his

lips to the sensitive skin under her ear, and circled her breast with his thumb. Teasing, tempting, until the tendrils of sensation returned.

'You must tell me if it hurts,' he said as he grasped her hips, anchoring her to him.

The arrows of sensation darted into her sex, devastating and demanding, echoing the same relentless rhythm as he drew out and sank back.

He rocked his hips, further, faster, nudging a place deep inside her, triggering a new tsunami of sensation.

Kasia sobbed. The storm was so much stronger and wilder this time, whipping at her skin, making every pulse point ache.

The pleasure overpowered her, battering her body and making her heart swell. She clung to him, the only solid object in the storm—just like before, her staggered mind cried, when he had cocooned her as the sandstorm had raged.

She screamed as he drove her over that final ledge and she plunged into the abyss, exquisite joy bursting everywhere.

She heard him shout as he collapsed on top of her, and his seed spurted into her womb.

CHAPTER SIX

WHAT HAVE YOU DONE?

Raif struggled to control the vicious punch of his heartbeat, and forced his fingers to release their death grip on Kasia's hips.

Shame and horror galloped on the heels of groggy afterglow as he withdrew from the tight clasp of her body and she flinched.

He had climaxed inside her, he had not intended to do so. But even as he grasped the humiliation of that, far worse was the knowledge that as soon as he had plunged into her to the hilt, and destroyed her virgin state, he had bound them both to a solemn covenant they could not break.

Why hadn't he taken the precautions he always took, to research a woman's background, to ask her the questions that would protect them both?

Because he had been desperate to have her, to claim her, something had been driving him as soon as he had stepped from the water this morning and seen her watching him, her eyes dazed with arousal. Maybe even before that. Had it been driving him as soon as he had spotted her, standing by her Jeep, her amber eyes sparkling with fear and defiance? Or as he had clawed his way back from the nightmare, coaxed by her soft voice and soothing fingers?

However, the beast had been awakened, and the destruction it had wrought—on his life, on hers—could not be undone.

Where he would have expected panic or even resentment, all he felt now was numb and strangely ambivalent about the inevitable repercussions.

Lying on his back, he stared at the ceiling of the tent, the rich fabrics, the dappled sunlight. Everything looked as it had when he had woken an hour ago, but now his whole life, and hers, would be different.

He had played with fate too many times before, he had known the risks always, had been so careful to guard against them, but with Kasia it had never even entered his head. Was that significant? Was there some comfort in knowing their fates had already been sealed?

'Is everything okay?'

He turned to find her watching him, her hands clasped against her breasts, the rings on her fingers glinting.

The surge of renewed yearning was unmistakeable even as his mind reeled with the implications of what had just transpired. He examined her artless expression, looking for signs of duplicity.

Had she planned this? To trap a prince? The broken-down Jeep, the gunshot, the long night as she'd helped him through the nightmare and then come to him at the waterside?

It seemed unlikely but plausible, until he remembered the storm.

No, she could not have planned that. Perhaps she had simply seen an opportunity and acted on it. Bitterness rose in his throat, but he swallowed it. Whatever her plots and schemes to get them here, he must take the lion's share of the blame. He was in charge of his own libido.

He was the one who had chosen to seduce her without knowing enough about her. And had lost control so spectacularly—as soon as he had pressed his face into the sweet seam of her sex and tasted her arousal.

Whatever her reasons, her motives, whichever

one of them was to blame, the consequences were stark and inescapable.

Shifting onto his side, he placed a hand on her cheek and hooked the riot of midnight hair behind her ear.

'I should not have taken you without protection,' he said, feeling humiliated all over again about his loss of control. 'There is no excuse. But a pregnancy hardly matters. Now we are to be wed.'

Her eyes popped wide. She scrambled into a sitting position, her brows shooting up her forehead.

'What?' she said, her tone raw with shock.

Interesting. Either she was the greatest actress he had ever seen, or she had not planned to trick him into marriage.

He took some solace from that. He had not been the only one to lose their head in the intense heat of their lovemaking.

He propped his head on his hand and studied her, convinced her shock was entirely genuine. And actually quite beguiling.

A delicious blush darkened her skin. She was exquisite. Perhaps this marriage would not be such a hardship.

'You were a virgin, Kasia,' he said, because she looked as if she was waiting for an explanation. Although he did not know why. However long she had been out of the kingdom, surely she must know of the sacred marriage laws of the Sheikhs, being Narabian. 'Even though I am a bastard, the blood of the royal house of Nawari flows in my veins,' he prompted, but still she looked clueless. 'So we must now be married.'

'But I can't marry you. I don't even know you. There won't be a baby, I'm right at the beginning of my cycle.'

He frowned. Okay, she looked more than shocked now, she looked panicked.

'A pregnancy is not the reason. Honour dictates it,' he continued, his throat closing on that one crucial word.

Honour. The one thing his father hadn't been able to steal from him. His honour had sustained him, through the loneliness, the pain, the starvation, the thirst, and the many other humiliations of being a boy without a people. Honour had ensured his survival. Had driven him to fight and fight until he had eventually triumphed. Not just finding a people, but becoming their Chief.

His honour meant everything to him and he

could not compromise it. Not for anything. Or anyone. Not even himself.

'I have taken your maidenhead,' he added. 'To maintain my honour, I must make you my wife and my consort.'

'But that's…' Kasia pulled in a few precious breaths, trying to stop herself from hyperventilating, not easy when she was edging towards hysteria. 'You can't be serious.'

Raif stared at her, his frown only making him more handsome. But she was so over the ripples of awareness making her sex throb.

'I am absolutely serious,' he said. 'We have no choice now.'

'Don't be ridiculous. There's always a choice.'

'Kasia.' He pressed his palm to her cheek, making the traitorous ripples worse. 'You must calm down…you are breathing too fast.'

She jerked her head back. She couldn't do this. She couldn't have a sensible conversation with him, especially not when he was looking at her with that pragmatic intensity.

She'd heard of the Law of Marriage of the Sheikhs. The ancient, archaic law was written into the country's scrolls. Scrolls she had studied along with Cat, once upon a time. She had once whispered about the old law furtively with her school friends. How it was a dream come true, a way for nobodies like them to become queens.

But it wasn't a dream any more, it was a nightmare.

The old law hadn't even occurred to her when she'd neglected to mention her virginity to Raif. Because she'd been far too caught up in the moment to think about anything. Not even contraception!

Standing up, she grabbed her T-shirt and tugged it on. She couldn't stay here and have this conversation. It took a while for her to find the armholes because she was shaking so hard.

Why hadn't she given a lot more thought to the repercussions of sleeping with Raif? He was clearly autocratic and arrogant. But what had been so exciting and seductive before she'd slept with him seemed fraught with disaster now.

She didn't want to be married to a stranger. She was supposed to be returning to Cambridge. This trip was to do preliminary research for a PhD in the eco-systems of the Narabian desert she was hoping to get funding for.

The intimacy of what they had shared would

be tarnished for ever by his callous demand that she succumb to his will. And for what? To maintain *his* honour? What about hers? She was a person, an individual, with her own free will. He couldn't ride roughshod over her future, her choices, because she'd been too caught up in the moment to warn him of her virginity.

She'd always promised herself that when she married, *if* she married, she would marry for love. She wanted the kind of fairy-tale romance Cat and Zane shared. She would never marry for duty or honour. And especially not to a man who didn't seem to know the difference between honour and duty and love.

She tugged on her shorts, suddenly desperate to escape the stifling tent, and the scene of her downfall, the lingering scent of sex only emphasising her stupidity.

If you slept with a man you didn't know, what the heck did you expect?

That had been her mistake. Not just trusting him, but trusting her own judgement. Because there was an element of what she'd done that made her remember her mother. The woman she hadn't seen since she was a girl.

'I can't be your mother any more, Kasia. Your grandmother will take good care of you.'

Her mother had abandoned her—because she could no longer bear the shame of having a child out of wedlock. Of being ostracised, vilified, damned for her pregnancy when she was alone. But Kasia had paid a far greater price, forced to grow up without her mother and battle for years the insecurities her absence had wrought—and all because of customs that punished people for loving in the wrong place, at the wrong time.

She did up the buttons of her shorts with clumsy fingers.

But as she went to leave the tent, he grasped her elbow.

'Where are you going?' he demanded.

'I need some air, and some time to think. And to wash.'

He'd put on his pants, thank goodness, but even so desire echoed in her sex as her gaze connected with his broad chest. She could see the red marks etched into the tattoo covering his shoulder where she had held him in the throes of passion.

What had she been thinking? Giving herself

to him, without a thought to any of the consequences?

'Kasia, you must not panic,' he said. 'This is frightening, I understand that. It is not a choice I would have made either,' he added, and she heard it then, the brittle note of judgement. Of accusation. Because she had been the one to keep her virginity a secret. 'But we are bound now.'

She could hear the steely determination in his voice.

But this was madness.

Why should they honour a code that had been set down hundreds of years before they were even born?

'I need to be alone for a bit,' she said. 'To consider all this. It's a lot to take in.'

He let his hand drop. Then he nodded. 'Okay, go to the pond and bathe, I will pack up here. We must travel to the Golden Palace before nightfall. Speak to your relatives.'

What? Panic clawed at her throat. 'But I don't have any relatives. Not since my grandmother died. Maybe if we just don't tell anyone about...'

'We cannot lie, that would be an even greater breach of honour,' he interrupted her, his frown deepening. 'If you have no relatives, then I will make the request for your hand to my brother. He is your employer, yes?'

He was moving too fast. She didn't want Zane and Cat to know what she'd done. She certainly didn't want to put them in the middle of this situation. They would, of course, support her decision. They weren't barbarians like Raif. But from the few times Prince Kasim had mentioned his half-brother it was obvious their relationship was problematic at best, and probably delicately balanced politically.

Good grief, her stupidity could start a new war.

The panic started to consume her.

Breathe—just breathe. And don't add any more drama than you absolutely have to.

She forced her lungs to function. Struggled to think. 'How far are we from the palace?' she asked, as a plan began to form in her head.

'A day's ride, to the north,' he said.

Oh, thank goodness.

'Okay,' she said as a strange calmness descended. 'I won't be too long.'

He grasped her arm. 'Do not despair, Kasia,' he said, his voice strained.

Her heart beat heavily against her ribs.

'We will find a way to make this work,' he said.

She nodded. Because she couldn't bring herself to speak.

Arguing with him was pointless. And she'd never been very good at disguising her feelings. If he knew how frantic she was, and how determined not to go through with this madness, he might not let her leave. But as she left, she couldn't resist glancing over her shoulder.

He stood, tall and proud and indomitable, trusting her to return.

She couldn't help hating herself a little as she headed towards the oasis, then doubled back through the trees. She didn't take any time to saddle his horse, simply used the corral's railings to mount the huge beast.

She hadn't ridden a horse for five years. But she had been an accomplished rider, as happy riding bareback as with a saddle. She prayed the ability hadn't left her as she kicked her bare heels into the horse's flanks. It snorted and reared, but she clung to its mane, her thigh muscles straining, the tenderness in her sex rubbing against the ridge of its spine.

She heard a shout and saw Raif run out of the tent, his face a mask of surprise and then fury as his stallion cleared the fence in one bound.

She dug her heels into the horse's sides, bent her head low over its neck and allowed the beast to have its head, managing to direct it towards the north as it flew over the rocks and towards the dunes.

Tears blurred her eyes, but she didn't look back this time.

She couldn't.

CHAPTER SEVEN

'KASIA, IF SOMETHING happened to you, however traumatic, you know you can tell me, right?'

Kasia stopped folding her recently unpacked clothes back into her suitcase. Her best friend, Catherine Ali Nawari Khan, stood with her back pressed against the door of Kasia's chamber, her face a picture of concern and distress.

Kasia nodded, determined to keep her voice calm and even. Or as calm and even as she could while the shame threatening to choke her since she'd arrived back at the palace an hour ago— heck, the shame that had been choking her since she'd galloped over the dunes and away from Raif's encampment—expanded another few centimetres.

'I just… I need to return to Cambridge.' It was cowardly, but it was the decision she'd made as she'd ridden Raif's horse.

She'd made a terrible mistake, not just sleeping with Raif but not telling him about her virginity.

She'd put them both in an impossible situation—a situation that could have constitutional implications for both countries if Raif continued his quest to marry her—and the only way to remedy the problem was to leave. And leave quickly, before he followed her to the palace.

She'd had a lucky break, spotting the column of SUVs that had been sent out to search for her only an hour after leaving his encampment. They'd driven her straight back to the palace, where Cat and Zane had been waiting. There had been hugs and kisses, tears of joy and relief, but then had come the questions. What had happened to her? How had she survived after her vehicle had been buried? Was she okay now? Did she need a doctor?

She'd devised a deliberately vague story. She'd been rescued by a tribesman who had taken her to his encampment and then loaned her his horse to return to the palace once the sandstorm had settled. But as soon as Zane had suggested they contact the man and thank him for his help, she had known her story wouldn't stand up to scrutiny for long. Not least because she suspected Zane knew she wasn't telling the whole truth. As soon as he'd tried to probe into the facts—

why hadn't the man given her a saddle, where were her shoes, where did they return the horse as it was clearly a valuable thoroughbred—Cat had intervened, insisting Kasia be given time to bathe and eat and recover from her ordeal. But she'd known it was only a matter of time before Cat's concern got the better of her.

Tears welled in her eyes. And Cat rushed across the chamber.

'Kasia—oh, my God. I knew something was wrong.' Gathering Kasia in her arms, she pressed a kiss to her forehead. 'Did the man who rescued you assault you, is that it? Whatever happened, it's not your fault, okay? You don't have to leave. We'll figure this out.'

Kasia shook her head, scrubbing away the tears of self-pity. She didn't deserve Cat's concern, didn't deserve her friend's comfort. And she was going to have to explain herself. Admit the humiliating mistakes she'd made while at the same time protecting everyone—Raif included—from the consequences.

'It's not that, he didn't assault me. In fact, it was the other way around. I actually... I shot him.'

Cat's eyebrows rose, but her gaze remained

supportive and direct. 'Is he dead?' she asked flatly.

'Goodness, no. He's okay, it was only a flesh wound.'

'All right,' Cat said. 'Well, that's good, I guess,' she added as if she weren't sure.

A raw chuckle burst out of Kasia's throat. 'How can it be good?' she said. 'I still shot him.'

'So what? If he was assaulting you, he got what he deserved,' Cat said, with complete pragmatism. And Kasia felt the tears scour her throat again.

'But he wasn't assaulting me,' she managed through the emotion thickening her throat. 'He was rescuing me from the sandstorm.'

'And you both survived, so it's all good,' Cat countered, gripping Kasia's arms. 'But something else happened, right? Something that's made you think you have to leave. And that's not—'

'I slept with him and now he's insisting we get married because I was a virgin.' The words burst out of Kasia's mouth in a flood, silencing Cat.

Her friend's eyebrows rose again. 'Okay,' she said. Her eyes narrowed as she stroked Kasia's arms in a gesture of solidarity Kasia wasn't sure she deserved.

'He definitely didn't coerce you into sleeping with him?' she asked.

'No, no, he didn't.'

If only he had, she might be able to let herself off the hook. But how could she, when she had been fully compliant, he'd given her a clear choice and she'd taken it. Heck, she hadn't just taken it, she'd jumped at it. 'It was absolutely, one hundred percent consensual.'

'Are you sure, Kaz?' Cat said gently. 'If he was your first, sometimes the issue of consent can be more complex.'

'Not this time. I wanted it to happen, very much,' she murmured in the interests of full disclosure, the humiliating truth making her cheeks burn. 'We'd spent the night together. He was exhausted and then he had this terrible nightmare... It was intimate and I totally objectified him. Because...' The flush climbed up to her hairline. 'He's really, really hot. And when we did it, I enjoyed it. A lot. In fact, I had two orgasms. I really couldn't have asked for a better experience for my first time. But afterwards...'

She sat down on the bed, scrubbed her hands

over her face, trying to erase the brutal memory of his face, so indomitable, so proud, so unyielding—and yet so trusting. 'He was adamant that his honour means we have to get married.' She clasped her hands together in her lap, remembering the leap of her stupidly romantic heart when he'd suggested it.

For a moment she'd actually considered it. She'd been shocked, yes, but a tiny part of her had been flattered and excited. Because that teenager who had spun romantic dreams about Raif before she'd ever met him had leapt out of hiding. But that adrenaline hit had been quickly followed by the cruel, harsh jolt of reality as soon as he'd begun to talk about honour and duty.

Marrying Prince Kasim, marrying anyone in these circumstances, would be totally wrong. However hot he was, or however many orgasms he could give her. They'd been thrown together by chance and, yes, they had sexual chemistry. But that was all they had. They didn't know each other.

And one of the few things Raif *did* know about her he didn't seem to think was relevant. She had a life plan, a plan that had changed and evolved since she was a little girl trying to justify her mother's abandonment, or that starry-eyed and over-excitable teenager working as a servant in the palace and dreaming of marrying a prince. And that life plan did not include an arranged marriage to a man who thought his honour was more important than her future, or his own.

'He can't force you to marry him,' Cat said, covering her clasped hands. 'Even if you went to him willingly and didn't tell him you were a virgin. If he follows you here and tries to insist, Zane will have his advisors explain the law to him. You don't even have to see him again if you don't want to. You certainly don't have to go back to England to avoid that confrontation.'

'I know,' she said. She turned her hands over and clutched Cat's.

Now would be the perfect time to tell Cat the whole truth, to reveal that the man she'd slept with was the ruler of the Kholadi and Zane's half-brother. And the reason he was demanding marriage was bound up in his bloodline and his legacy and the responsibilities he had to his position—it wasn't just a generic obsession with Narabia's more traditional and outdated customs.

But she couldn't tell Cat.

Not only was she hopelessly ashamed of her

behaviour, she knew if she told Cat, and by extension Zane, they would still back her to the hilt. But it would put them in an impossible position. Especially given Zane's strained relationship with Raif.

She'd screwed up, and the only way she could see to fix it was to leave. If she returned to the UK, Raif wouldn't follow her there. It would let them both off the hook—erasing the problem and releasing him from an obligation he didn't want. He would no longer be bound by the ancient law if the woman he had compromised, or thought he had compromised, was thousands of miles away. Surely even *his* honour wouldn't dictate that he leave the desert, leave his people to venture out into a world he knew nothing about to track down a woman he'd had an ill-advised one-morning stand with?

'I'd rather just go back to the UK,' she said. 'And forget this ever happened.' Not that she ever would be able to forget Raif, she thought miserably, as the swelling in her throat was joined by the hot throb of reaction in her sex.

He was going to be a hard act to follow. But that's what happened when you chose to lose your virginity to the man of your dreams, and he lived up to every single one of them.

'Are you sure?' Cat said, her eyes shadowed with concern.

'Yes, I'm positive. If the man follows me here...' There was always the possibility that Raif wouldn't come to the Golden Palace, but from the furious frown on his face the last time she'd seen him, she wasn't taking that chance. If nothing else, she felt sure he would want to get his beautiful horse back. She ought to have at least a couple of days' grace as he only had the small pack pony to ride and would have to return to the Kholadi encampment first to get a new mount. 'It'll be easier for everyone concerned if you can explain I'm no longer here. I know it's cowardly but I—'

'Stop saying that, Kasia. There's not a cowardly bone in your body. I totally understand if you want to avoid this guy,' she added, patting Kasia's arm. 'I'll help you pack. Then I'll arrange a car to take you to the airport in Kallah—we can book you on the flight out tonight.'

'Thanks.' Kasia smiled at her friend, so pathetically grateful for Cat's stalwart support she had to swallow down another wave of tears. 'Will Zane be okay with that?'

'He'll have questions, I expect,' Cat said. 'But he trusts my judgement and he trusts you, too, Kasia. And no way would he make you face this guy if you don't want to, okay?'

Kasia nodded. 'Thanks.'

Cat smiled. 'At least it's good to know you got two orgasms out of him before he turned into a jerk.'

Kasia forced herself to smile back. 'And they were spectacular ones, to be fair.'

Cat laughed. 'There you go. Spectacular orgasms are never bad.'

But Kasia's heart shrank in her chest as Cat dashed off to make the travel arrangements and left her to finish packing.

Zane trusted Cat's judgement because he adored his queen. Theirs was the kind of relationship Kasia had always hoped to emulate. It was one of the other reasons she had never dated seriously in Cambridge. Because she'd wanted what Zane and Cat had—before she'd been hijacked by her own pheromones.

But it wasn't just her pheromones that were to blame for this disaster.

The bedrock of a relationship like Zane and Cat's was trust and honesty—something Kasia had failed at the very first time she was tested.

Somehow she doubted Zane would trust her once he found out to whom she'd given her virginity so thoughtlessly. In fact, he might well hate her a little if there was any political fallout from this mess. She may well have soured her relationship with the Sheikh—a man she had always admired a great deal and whose respect meant a lot.

But why did it hurt so much more to know the person who would probably hate her most was Raif?

CHAPTER EIGHT

'KASIA SALAH—I need to speak to her. Now.'

Raif controlled the fury that had been building for four days now, and held onto the curse word lodged in his throat as the woman standing at the gate of the Golden Palace's women's quarters trembled visibly but still refused to open the damn gate.

He didn't bully women. But this was intolerable. He'd arrived fifteen minutes ago and he still hadn't been able to locate Kasia.

Following a short ride and a very long walk to the nearest Kholadi encampment, he'd been forced to rest overnight to get his strength back after a bout of vomiting before he'd been able to make the two-day ride to Zafari.

A pain in his right side had developed during the journey. And he'd had to stop several times to recuperate—turning the two-day ride into three. Somehow in the midst of this titanic mess he'd managed to pick up a very persistent stomach bug as well.

He probably should have waited until he had completely recovered from it before making the journey. But the urge to find Kasia and confront her had been stronger than his common sense.

She'd run out on him. Stolen his horse. And all after promising to consider his proposal of marriage. He should have expected it. No one was ever as guileless as they appeared. He should never have trusted her.

'I'm sorry, Prince Kasim, but she is not here,' the girl said.

'Then where the hell is she?' The shout rang out as his smouldering temper burst into flames and the aching pain ground in his gut. The girl cowered.

'Kasim, I've only just been informed of your arrival. We hadn't expected you.'

Raif swung round to see his brother striding across the courtyard towards him, followed by two of his advisors.

Terrific. Just what I need—a political delegation to slow this process down even more.

His brother clasped his hand, giving him a jolt

that seemed to knife into his gut. Raif struggled not to flinch.

'It's good to see you, as always, brother.' While Zane's smile was tight—he was probably wondering what Raif had been doing at the gates of the women's quarters, shouting at one of his staff—it looked genuine, which only annoyed Raif more.

He was far too irritable and out of sorts right now to make the effort to pretend a brotherly bonhomie he didn't feel.

He respected his half-brother, had been forced to acknowledge over the last ten years that Zane was a good Sheikh. But they were hardly friends. Even if Zane could overlook the difference in their upbringing—as the legitimate, wanted son of the old Sheikh and the son he had never acknowledged—Raif could not.

For some reason, Zane always acted as if their tainted past didn't exist, often going to extraordinary lengths to deny the strained nature of their sibling relationship.

The only time Raif had managed to get a rise out of Zane had been five years ago when Zane had arrived at the Kholadi camp with the academic he had hired to write a book about the kingdom. Raif had sensed the attraction between Zane and Catherine Smith and had decided to have some fun at his brother's expense, mercilessly flirting with the young woman during their evening meal and then assigning her the same tent as Zane, even though Zane had insisted they be accommodated separately. Raif had won that round. Zane had been furious with him, but unable to show it because he had been maintaining the fiction he wasn't sleeping with his beautiful biographer. But the last laugh had eventually been on Raif when the two of them had married a scant three weeks later and Catherine had become Zane's queen.

Since then, and for the sake of diplomacy, Raif had made an effort to be civil to his brother. But right now he just wanted to see Kasia, to talk to her, to find out why she'd run from him and to impress upon her again the reality of their situation. And to have this damn pain in his gut go away.

He did not have the time or the patience to deal with his brother.

'Come, Kasim, and have coffee with me.' Zane finally let go of Raif's hand and held out his arm, directing him away from the gates. 'We can catch up.'

'Okay,' he said, struggling to keep his voice low despite his rising temper. His tender stomach ached after the endless ride through the desert, his skin felt clammy, his head was pounding as if Zarak had kicked him in the temple. But he would have to humour his brother before he returned to discover where Kasia was. Because he had no desire to explain his situation with the girl.

Never show weakness, that was the motto he lived by. And especially not to the man who his father had decided mattered, when Raif did not.

He knew that the way he had been treated by their father was not Zane's fault—both of them had been pawns in Tariq's political manoeuvres—but still he couldn't shake the feeling that where Zane was concerned he always had to be better, stronger, and smarter to prove himself worthy.

Sweat trickled down his back beneath his robe, his mind fogging with frustration and exhaustion, the pain in his right side making it hard for him to walk. But as they approached the ornate silver doors to the Sheikh's private chambers, the pain sliced agonisingly into his gut.

He bent over, his grunt of agony echoing through the corridor.

'Kasim, what the…?'

He could hear Zane's voice through the wild-fire spreading through his body.

He locked his knees.

Stay upright, dammit.

But his legs refused to obey him, dissolving beneath him like sand.

The dull thud reverberated through him as he went down hard on his knees.

Zane's arms wrapped around Raif's torso as he tried to catch him, but it was already too late and darkness rushed towards him.

'Malik, get the doctor for Prince Kasim. Now.'

'My name is Raif,' he corrected his brother. 'Not Kasim.' The words were expelled on a final tortured breath as he crashed head first into the abyss.

Raif blinked up at the luxurious velvet drapes, the scent of jasmine echoing in his groin.

My angel? Where is my angel?

The powerful sense of *déjà vu* overwhelmed him, but as he turned his head, he saw a middle-aged woman beside the bed in a white coat, who stood up and leaned over him. But as she spoke in a stream of Narabian—while checking his temperature and his vital signs—the deep sense of disappointment became a hollow ache.

She isn't here. Not this time. She ran away from you.

'Where am I?' he asked in English, his throat raw with thirst as he tried to dispel the miserable inadequacy that had plagued him as a child.

'You are in His Divine Majesty's private chambers, Prince Kasim,' the doctor replied. 'Nurse, tell the Sheikh that Prince Kasim is conscious.'

A young man seated at the end of the bed rushed from the room.

Damn. Damn. Damn.

He had collapsed, fainted like a fool, in front of his brother. Humiliation washed over him. He shifted, tried to lift himself, clenching his teeth against the dull pain in his stomach. And the pinch in his forearm as the movement tugged on the drip taped to his skin.

He needed to get the hell out of this bed. He was lying here naked and exposed, like an invalid.

But the doctor placed a hand on his sternum, finding it pathetically easy to press him into the sheets—he had no more strength than a new-born baby.

'You must not move, Prince Kasim,' she said, the pity in her voice increasing his humiliation. 'You have a lot more healing to do. We had to operate as there was an infection.'

Operate? Infection?

He noticed for the first time the stars in the dark sky glinting through the elegant carved wooden screens on the chamber's window. Hadn't he arrived here in the afternoon? How could it already be night-time? Had he been lying here for hours?

'How...?' he rasped, the effort to speak exhausting him. He cleared his throat. 'How long have I been here?' he managed.

'Two weeks, Your Highness,' she said.

Two weeks!

Horror replaced his humiliation as a flush of shame engulfed him.

He'd been helpless, laid out like a child, relying on his brother's charity for two whole weeks?

'Raif, you're finally awake.'

Zane strode into the chamber, the picture of health and vitality, the bastard.

Except he isn't the bastard—you are.

But why had Zane called him by his Kholadi name? Raif frowned, confusion adding to his growing misery. His tired mind struggled to grasp the implications. The new intimacy between them was almost as disturbing as knowing he'd been at his brother's mercy for two weeks.

'How is he?' Zane addressed the doctor.

She reeled off a string of jargon and he realised he had been operated on because of a burst appendix. That he had nearly died. Then she told his brother he was on the mend.

But he didn't feel on the mend, he felt broken. And it had nothing to do with the tenderness still lingering in his gut.

How could he have sunk this low? To have risked his life. To follow a woman. A woman who didn't want him. Who had run from him and had no respect for his honour or her own. And how could he still want her?

The burning shame in his chest began to change into something more fortifying. He was limp with exhaustion, yes, but that would pass, and when it did he would find Kasia Salah. And he would make her pay for bringing him to this.

After more admonitions for him to remain in

bed and focused on his recovery, the doctor left the room, leaving him alone with his brother.

Zane sat in the chair the doctor had vacated and leaned forward. 'So, Kasim…' He paused. 'Sorry, I mean Raif.' He folded his fingers together, levelling Raif with a stare that brooked no argument. 'Why didn't you tell me years ago you prefer to use the name Raif? And why the hell did you ride all the way here in agony?'

CHAPTER NINE

Hey, Kaz,

I hope all's good with you, and you're over your hot night with the mystery tribesman. You'll be glad to know no one has turned up here to claim your hand in marriage, so I hope you'll consider coming back for a visit again very soon.

Why haven't you been in touch? Six texts saying precisely nothing in four weeks doesn't count btw—just in case you were wondering.

All's good on the home front.

Zane has bought Kaliah her own pony and begun teaching her to ride. Personally, I think five-going-on-fifteen is too young, but I've been overruled by both of them, as usual! I include photos of her on her horse for her Auntie Kaz, at her insistence.

William, meanwhile, continues to be an

absolute terror. I can't believe he still isn't sleeping through the night and he's nearly two. Neither can Zane, who says he's going to get tough on his son, then doesn't...

His Divine Majesty is a complete push-over where his children are concerned, and unfortunately for us both they know it.

We got a surprise visit from Prince Kasim— over a month ago now—who promptly collapsed and had to be nursed back to health. He turned up unannounced and without the usual honour guard of tribesmen. He left us last week.

He had a burst appendix and had to be operated on. When he finally came round he steadfastly refused to talk about why he had come to visit us in the first place and ridden for three days in agony to get here.

I told him he was definitely taking the whole 'Bad-Boy Sheikh' thing a bit too far. He did not see the funny side—having apparently had a major sense of humour failure. As it turns out, desert princes make the worst possible patients! Who knew?

The doctor also noticed he had a fresh scar

on his arm from what she thought might be a bullet wound—which made me think of your mystery tribesman. But I'm guessing your guy couldn't possibly be Prince Kasim—or Raif, as Zane now calls him, for no reason I can fathom—because you totally would not have kept the juiciest piece of girl talk in a millennium a secret from your BFF, now, would you?

Give me a call soon and let me know how everything is going.

I miss you.

All my love

C xox

KASIA RE-READ THE handwritten letter, which had arrived that morning, for the sixth time in as many minutes. Tears stung her eyes and dripped onto the photo Cat had sent of her five-year-old daughter. Kaliah's wide grin showed off her missing front tooth as she sat on her new pony.

Kasia wiped the moisture off her cheeks and stuffed the letter back into its envelope. Then, with trembling fingers, pinned the print of Kaliah and her pony onto the board above her desk.

Raif had been seriously ill for three weeks because of her. He'd only just recovered. How would she ever forgive herself?

Guilt and nausea roiled in her stomach, making the fatigue that had been dragging her down for a week weigh on her shoulders like a slab of concrete.

Placing the letter in the top drawer of the desk, she fished out the cardboard box she'd bought from the chemist's yesterday.

She turned the pregnancy testing kit over in her hands and read the instructions. Again.

She couldn't put it off any longer. Cat's letter and the devastating news about Raif's illness and recovery was a sign. A sign she had to start taking responsibility for her actions. She was convinced her symptoms were psychosomatic— even though he hadn't pulled out during their lovemaking, she *had* been at the very beginning of her cycle. And her period was only two days overdue, which wasn't that unusual for her.

This obsession with her so-called symptoms— the mild nausea, the tender breasts, the emotional roller-coaster, the bone-deep fatigue that had hit every evening for a week—was some weird psychological hangover from her time in the desert, which she hadn't been able to get out of her head.

Every night she dreamed of him. Not just the vivid erotic dreams that woke her up sweaty and unfulfilled, her skin prickling with sensation, her heart thundering, her clitoris slick and swollen from the far-too-real memory of his tongue stroking her to orgasm. But also the much more unsettling visions of him when they had ridden together through the storm, when he'd cried out in his sleep and the harsh frown of disbelief on his face as she'd galloped away from him.

And now Cat's letter had made all those symptoms that much more pronounced.

Something had happened to her at the oasis, something profound and life-changing that went beyond the sex. Something she wasn't going to be able to come to terms with until she made absolutely sure, once and for all, that she wasn't pregnant with Raif Kasim Ali Kholadi Khan's child.

Emotion caused a lump to form in her throat as she walked into the small en suite bathroom of her room in the hall of residence.

After unwrapping the test stick, it took her

several agonising minutes to manage to pee on it. She placed it on the vanity unit and washed her hands, then sat on the toilet seat and set the stopwatch on her smartphone to the required two minutes to get the result.

Which turned in to the longest two minutes of her entire life.

The questions she didn't want to answer that were roaring around in her head were almost as deafening as the sandstorm she and Raif had survived all those weeks ago.

She should have done this yesterday when she'd bought the test. Why hadn't she? Was it because she didn't want to have a pregnancy confirmed, or the much more disturbing thought that she did? Why would she want to be pregnant by a man she barely knew? A man who appeared to comprehensively lack the sensibilities she had always dreamed of finding in a life partner? Was she really that needy and lonely and insecure that she yearned to have a child, whatever the circumstances of its birth?

But the combination of anticipation and dread tangling with the nausea in her stomach didn't feel as if it was just a result of her long-held desire that one day she wanted to be a mother. No, these complex urges were not generic or anonymous, but intrinsically linked to Raif and the intense time they had shared together, every single moment of which she kept reliving.

Her phone buzzed and she shrieked.

Okay, it's official—you are actually going insane.

But when she looked at the stopwatch she realised her two minutes weren't up yet. Instead, a message had appeared on the phone screen from the sponsorship team at Devereaux College. She frowned as she read the message.

Ms Salah,

We've received a request that you attend a black-tie reception tonight in London at eight p.m.

The guest of honour Mr R Khan —a billionaire businessman from your home region, I understand—is thinking of funding a scholarship programme at Devereaux. We would very much appreciate it if you would agree to attend this event so that you can discuss your current research with him. We are hopeful that a scholarship programme of this nature, if agreed, will help fund your PhD.

A car will be made available to transport you to London.

Regards

Alice Evershot

Devereaux Scholarship Team

The request was not at all what she needed right now. But she would have to attend the event tonight and make a good impression—any chance of getting her PhD funded was not something she could afford to pass up.

But when the alarm on her phone buzzed again, making her jump, she realised Alice Evershot's request had managed to take her mind off Raif and that one seminal night in the desert for ten full seconds—a record for the last month.

Drawing a breath into her lungs, she reached for the test stick, finally ready to face what the rest of her life might hold.

The breath was released in a shattered gasp as she read the result.

CHAPTER TEN

KASIA RE-READ HER notes as the car drew into the forecourt of a landmark hotel on London's Strand.

She stuffed the creased pages into her clutch bag and stared up at the silver-plated sign on the hotel's Art Deco frontage.

She was no stranger to luxury, having lived in the Golden Palace for as long as she could remember before moving to the UK, but—as a uniformed doorman stepped forward to open the heavy glass doors with a flourish and the porter led her through the lobby area resplendent in Edwardian marble and gilt-edged antique furniture—the grandeur took her breath away.

But, then, she'd been struggling to catch her breath all day, ever since reading the results of the pregnancy test.

She pressed a hand to her stomach, her palm sliding over the sleek red silk of the cocktail dress she'd found at a second-hand boutique in Cambridge that afternoon.

She was going to have Prince Kasim's baby. Raif's baby.

Her breath seized all over again as it had so many times since that morning.

So many uncertainties and challenges awaited her in the weeks and months ahead—and most of them seemed insurmountable at the moment.

Somehow she would have to tell Cat and Zane that Raif was the mystery tribesman. That his burst appendix was her fault. And eventually she would have to tell the desert prince himself about her pregnancy. He had a right to know he was going to become a father.

But all the reasons she had run from him and her homeland a month ago still applied. In fact, this development would make them even tougher to negotiate.

Raif had obviously decided not to pursue marriage once he had recovered, but he might well insist on it again when he discovered she was going to have his child. And how could she expect Cat and Zane to protect her from such a union when they might be conflicted, too? Especially Zane. After all he had insisted on marriage with Cat when she had become pregnant with *his* child. And Raif was his brother. Where would his loyalties lie? With her—however close she was to the Royal household—or with his own blood?

Overwhelmed didn't even begin to describe how she had been feeling about her condition ever since she'd seen the fat red plus sign. But despite all the questions and uncertainties, and the impact her baby would have on her academic career, the one thing she did know was that she wanted this baby. Raif's baby.. Very much.

She pushed the recurring questions to one side, or tried to, her clutch purse instinctively guarding her belly as the porter directed her through the inlaid silver doors of a lavish ballroom.

At least she had time to consider her options. Once she'd told Cat, she could talk the situation through with her best friend, figure out how best to break the news to Raif and when. Luckily, having Raif thousands of miles away gave her a buffer zone from having to confront anything before she was ready.

Right now, all she had to do was absorb the surreal joy at the prospect of becoming a mother in approximately eight months' time. Something she'd always dreamed of being. Maybe she wouldn't have planned for it to happen this way, but once she got over the shock—and worked out how and when to tell the father to avoid an all-out war on the Narabian peninsula—she could embrace the awe. Luckily, she'd always been a positive, self-sufficient person who knew how to think on her feet—or she would be, once she got over the feeling that the rug had just been pulled out from under said feet.

As she stepped into the crowd of elegantly dressed guests—the men in tuxedos and most of the women in ballgowns—she recited her speech again in her head while searching for the Devereaux College representative she had been told would be there to introduce her to the potential donor.

She walked through the room, faking confidence. With her wild hair tamed and curled after an hour spent with her trusty curling irons, the high heels she'd borrowed from another post-grad student and her newish dress, at least she knew she looked good.

She took a moment to calm her erratic heart-beat. She needed to remember the speech she'd worked on to charm the billionaire donor she wanted to impress. Securing funding for her PhD was very important now, or her future—and her baby's future—would be even more insecure.

French doors lined one side of the high-ceilinged hall, affording the guests a stunning vista of the Thames at twilight. Big Ben and the Houses of Parliament were spotlighted from the balcony at the far end, while the London Eye lit up the Georgian splendour of the old County Hall building across the water.

The clink of glasses and the hum of polite conversation covered the delicacy of a Brahms concerto being played by a string quartet in one corner while discreet wait staff passed around gold trays of canapés and vintage Champagne.

The scene really was breathtaking. Who knew there was this much money—and glamour—in university funding initiatives?

'Miss Salah? You made it.' The familiar face of one of Alice Evershot's assistants popped up beside her.

'Yes. Hello, I—'

'Come this way.' The young man interrupted her attempt at polite introductions to direct her through the crowd. 'Mr Khan is impatient to meet you and I really don't want to keep him waiting any longer,' he said as he moved swiftly through the throng.

She had to speed up to keep pace with the young man. Her heartbeat became erratic again as they stepped out of the French doors. A man stood at the far end of the balcony alone, in an expertly tailored tuxedo, his tall muscular frame silhouetted against the Houses of Parliament. This was the donor? She'd expected someone much older. Even from behind this man looked young and fit.

And oddly familiar.

It's not Raif. Are you mad? You have to forget about him, at least for tonight.

Goosebumps ran riot over her skin. Which was strange. It was a warm late-summer evening and there was no breeze to speak of.

'Mr Khan,' the assistant called from behind her. 'I have located Ms Salah for you.'

The music and laughter and the hum of polite conversation was drowned out by the thud of her own heartbeat and the low rumble of the traffic along the Embankment as she walked towards the donor with the assistant at her side.

Her heels echoed in the night, but her heartbeat became deafening. Even his stance reminded her of Raif. So proud, so arrogant. His close-cropped black hair shone blue in the lights from the reception.

He hadn't turned, and she wondered if he was annoyed she had arrived a little late as his stance seemed tense. Not a great start to this schmoozing initiative.

She swallowed down the strange feeling of unreality as she approached him, but the goose-bumps continued to run riot over the bare skin of her arms. And a heavy weight sank low into her abdomen. Hadn't he heard the assistant?

'Mr Khan, I'm so sorry I'm late,' she said.

The man turned at last, bringing his face into the light. And dark chocolate eyes bored into her soul.

Recognition slammed into her and she staggered to a stop.

A giddy rush of desire followed as she devoured his rugged features, the thick brows drawn into a sharp line, the clean-shaven jaw revealing the tense muscle bunching in his cheek.

It can't be him. I'm hallucinating.

Her hand covered her stomach as if she could shield the child already growing inside her from the shock.

His shuttered gaze roamed over her, entitled, assured, alight with barely suppressed fury... And undisguised desire.

Her breath cut off, the weight plunging down to throb and ache in the sweet spot between her thighs. Her already tender breasts squeezed into hard peaks, her nipples thrusting against the satin.

'Raif?' Her mouth formed the word, while everything inside her rebelled.

The assistant began to make the introductions but she couldn't hear a word of what the eager young man was saying. And it seemed neither could Raif, his gaze fixed firmly on her burning face.

He's not real. He can't be. This isn't happening.

How could the Desert Prince be standing in front of her, handsome and indomitable and completely at home at an elite high-society reception in the heart of London, his pristine white shirt making his skin look even darker?

His lips lifted on one side in a sarcastic half-smile, both sensual and brittle. And the memories she had been holding so carefully at bay for four weeks bombarded her all at once.

'Hello, Kasia.' His rough, accented voice scraped over every one of her nerve endings.

The assistant stopped talking abruptly, then cleared his throat. 'Mr Khan, I had no idea you already knew Ms Salah.'

What are you doing here?

Her mind screamed. The painful breath left her lungs as she struggled to engage with the evidence of her eyes.

This was Raif, but not as she had known him. This man was still the Desert Prince, she could feel his strength, his authority, still pulsing under his skin, barely contained. But he looked as comfortable in the tailored suit as he had on an Arabian stallion.

'We have met before,' he said, stepping closer as he glanced at the assistant. 'I wish to speak to Ms Salah in private, if that is all right with her,' he said, his intense gaze challenging her to deny him this intimacy.

But how could she? He'd nearly died on her account. Racing across a desert to find her when he'd been gravely ill. And he was the father of her child.

'Ms Salah?' the assistant said, clearly confused now. 'Is that all right with you?'

'Yes,' she murmured, as sensation rippled over her skin and gathered in her sex, telling her, in case she had ever doubted it, that she still wanted him.

The assistant left swiftly, probably feeling like the fifth wheel he was, and closed the balcony doors behind him.

'Why are you here?' she asked, at last.

'I think you know,' he said, stepping closer, filling her lungs with the intoxicating scent of him—man and musk and clean pine soap. 'I deserve answers. And I intend to get them.'

His chin lifted and she heard voices behind her. A couple had walked out onto the balcony. Her heart bounced into her throat as he swore under his breath at the interruption. 'It's like a train station here,' he said. 'Will you come with me to my suite?'

She should say no, she was still in shock from seeing him again, and going to his suite would hardly enhance her reputation. But her body refused to yield, the yearning to be with him again almost painful as she imagined him near death in Narabia.

She nodded.

'Good,' he murmured, then captured her hand

and marched down the balcony. Entering the ballroom, he hauled her behind him. She had to lengthen her stride to keep up as he made his way through the crowd.

'Mr Khan, Ms Salah, how is the discussion going?' The young assistant rushed towards them, blocking their path to the exit.

'Very well,' Raif replied, impatience rippling through him as he was forced to stop. 'I am inclined to agree to fund the scholarship initiative,' he added to the assistant, disconcerting Kasia again.

Raif was the billionaire donor? *Really?* But how? And why? The Kholadi were a nomadic tribe, they had no wealth, no riches, their ancient lifestyle and customs based on barter and trade, not money. Or that's what she had always believed as a teenager.

'That's wonderful,' the assistant said, his cheeks flushing with pleasure. 'Can I get you both a drink?'

Raif tensed, and she could sense his frustration at the assistant's interruption almost choking him now, but instead of demanding the man get out of their way, he turned to Kasia. 'Your choice, Ms Salah,' he murmured. 'Would you like a drink?'

The words shot through her, reminding her of another choice he'd given her a month ago. A choice that had ended in the baby now growing inside her.

Despite his fury with her, his obvious sense of grievance, he was giving her a choice again. A choice she had accused him of denying her all those weeks ago.

A choice to escape his questions, or face up to this discussion—a discussion she had avoided the last time by running away.

Gathering her courage, she turned to the assistant. 'It's okay, Devon,' she said. 'We're going to go to Mr Khan's suite to discuss the proposals for the scholarship in more depth.'

Devon looked delighted. 'Wonderful. Don't let me stand in your way, then,' he said, stepping aside to let them pass. 'I'll let Ms Evershot know about your discussion,' he shouted after them as Raif led her through the crowd.

But Alice Evershot and the scholarship initiative flew out of Kasia's mind as Raif marched her out of the ballroom and up a sweeping staircase to the next level. Nodding at two bodyguards, he shoved open a door marked 'Royal Suite'.

She found herself in a luxury suite of rooms, the sitting room decorated in cream silk and dark mahogany. The panoramic view of the river from a large terrace beyond the suite was even more spectacular than the one from the ballroom below.

But as he let go of her wrist and slammed the door behind them, it wasn't the view that made her breathless.

Her whole body began to shake as she wrapped her arms around her waist.

He tugged his bow-tie loose and shrugged off his jacket, throwing it over the back of a three-seater sofa. Then he undid the top buttons of his shirt. She could see the edge of the serpent tattoo on his collarbone, the red and black ink coiling over his skin—and the forceful reminder of the night they had spent together brought with it another devastating truth.

He nearly died.

The information in Cat's letter that morning reverberated in her skull.

His pursuit of her had nearly killed him. No

wonder he wanted answers. But little did he know she had much more to answer for now.

'I'm so sorry,' she blurted out, backing away from him as he stalked towards her across the silk carpet.

'What for?' he asked.

'Cat wrote to me and told me how ill you were. That's because of me. I never should have run away like that, but I never meant—'

'Stop.' He pressed his hand to her mouth to silence her. Then captured her waist and pressed her back against the silk-papered wall of the suite. Instead of fury she saw the same riot of emotions on his face that were churning in her stomach—desire, confusion. But most of all need.

He took his hand away from her mouth.

'That's not because of you.' His forehead touched hers as his fingers gripped the silk of her dress. Reaction shuddered through him and echoed through her. Powerful and unstoppable. 'I should not have ridden through the pain for three days to get to you,' he murmured, his lips touching her earlobe.

He had ridden for *three days* to follow her? Risking his health in the process? Agony and ecstasy echoed through her body. Why did his actions seem romantic, instead of foolhardy or simply insane? Maybe because no man had ever cared about her enough to do such a thing?

His lips closed over her earlobe. She arched against him, instinctively encouraging the contact, her whole body revelling in the response as he buried his face in her neck. The remembered ache became real and vivid again and a tortured moan escaped her lips.

'It was madness and I paid for it,' he said, his warm breath sending shivers down her back, his palms rubbing her waist, the silk feeling like sandpaper against too-sensitive skin. 'I'm not here for an apology.'

She pressed her palms to his jaw to draw his head up. His dark gaze was tortured, as tortured as she felt.

'Then why are you here, Raif?' she asked, around the knot of fear and joy in her throat.

'Because I still want you, dammit. And I can't make it stop.'

It wasn't what Raif had meant to say. Not even close. But once the words left his lips, he knew they were true.

He'd spent the last week—after finally managing to convince his brother and his brother's doctor and his brother's wife that he was fit enough to travel again—catching up on the million and one things that had been neglected during his illness while also planning this event.

He'd wanted to lure her to London. Had used the promise of funding a scholarship programme to control the interaction and had settled on a public meeting to ensure he didn't lose his temper with her. Where Kasia Salah was concerned, he already knew his ability to be rational had deserted him long ago. Why had he seduced her, why had he tried to bully her into marriage— a knee-jerk reaction that he had regretted after the week spent in his brother's home with far too much time to think—and why had he put his pride and dignity and his health in jeopardy by pursuing her to the Golden Palace like a lunatic?

But as soon as he'd seen her again, the fury, the desire for revenge had turned into something a great deal more volatile.

In a grubby T-shirt and shorts she had been exquisite; in the silky red dress, which clung to her slender body, accentuating her high, full breasts and subtle curves, she was irresistible.

Her amber eyes, the lids smudged with glittery make-up, had met his and all he'd wanted to do was feast on her again, and make her moan. His tongue had thickened at the thought of licking the side of her neck. His fingertips had itched to find the pins holding the waterfall of curls on top of her head and pull them out until the vibrant mass fell into his palms. And the blood had surged straight to his groin, the desire to pump into her tight heat all but unbearable.

But more than that, and somehow worse, when she'd searched his face a moment ago, her eyes filled with shame and remorse, he had wanted to take her distress away. To protect her, to hold her, to take all the blame, when this situation was more her fault than his.

He'd made some stupid knee-jerk decisions, but she'd made more.

Her gaze widened with shock at his revelation, but the flare of desire told him all he needed to know.

Why was he complicating this? He had planned this meeting precisely to take this yearning, this longing away.

This was about sex—it had always been about sex. Maybe it had become complicated by her virginity and his illness. But now he was here, in London, and fully recovered, why should they be bound by an ancient ritual that meant nothing outside their homeland?

He'd tried to do the right thing, to honour his culture and to honour her—and to show her the respect due to her after some warped reading of what he had discovered about his mother's situation with his father several years ago.

But this situation was not the same as what had happened to the woman who had died giving birth to him. A woman who he had refused to think about, until Zane had insisted he read his father's journals.

Given his overreaction to Kasia's virginity, he wished he had never read the damn journals. Never discovered the truth. What did the circumstances of his birth have to do with who he had become anyway? He had never known the girl his father had exploited and his father had never acknowledged him, her child.

The truth had messed with his head, his sense of self, or he would not have made that stupid declaration about his honour, about having to marry Kasia. And even if an elemental part of who he was and had always been made him feel responsible for her virginity, and the loss of it, surely the point was that her virginity had no bearing on where they were now.

They were both a continent away from their culture, those rituals. The Law of Marriage of the Sheikhs did not apply in London, even if it ever had in that tent.

Kasia Salah had chosen to leave Narabia five years ago. After four years of living—and succeeding—in this world as well as his own, he knew how it worked, too. So why should he not treat her as he would any other woman he desired? She certainly looked the part in that provocative dress and her high heels.

She wasn't a virgin any more. And they weren't in the desert now.

He cradled her cheek, traced with his thumb the spot where her pulse fluttered against her collarbone and adjusted his stance so she could feel the thick erection and know exactly what she still did to him.

'The only question I need an answer to is do you still want me, Kasia? If not, you can leave now, and I will never seek you out again.'

It was a promise that it would kill him to keep, if he had read the flare of arousal, her passionate response to him wrong. But he *would* keep it. Because he wasn't the barbarian she had assumed he was. And he'd debased himself enough already to have her—not just travelling across a desert in his frenzy, and leaving himself at the mercy of his brother, but travelling across an ocean, across continents. He hadn't been able to get her out of his head for a whole month; his whole damn life had been thrown into turmoil because of his association with her.

But he didn't *need* Kasia, he just wanted her.

'Answer me,' he demanded. 'Do you still want me?'

Her breathing was ragged, her features tense, but he could already see the truth in her eyes, and the rush of arousal surged.

'I… I *do* still want you,' she said at last, her tone anxious but not unsure.

It was enough.

'Good,' he murmured in the Kholadi dialect as he bent to scoop her into his arms.

He marched through the suite's living area and into the palatial bedroom—the light from streetlamps outside flickering over her dark skin. He didn't turn on the bedroom light before stripping off her clothes then tearing off his own. He watched her watch him as he rolled a condom on the massive erection.

He would have her now and he would find a way to keep her, for as long as it took to feed this hunger and take this inexplicable yearning away.

And then they would part, and he would never have to feel so unsettled or desperate again.

He cupped her breasts, licked the areolas, then sucked the swollen peaks into his mouth as he tested her readiness with his fingers. She sobbed and arched into his hand, the feel of her slick folds, the swollen nub enough to drive him a little crazy as he grasped her thighs, positioned her hips. He sank to the hilt in one thrust. Her muscles contracted around him in spontaneous orgasm. He set up a deep driving rhythm, wanting her to come again, to come apart in his arms.

He wasn't that little boy any more, alone and afraid, marked and then discarded by his own father and made to feel he was nothing.

He was a man, a chief, a prince, a business tycoon and everything he wanted he could have—if he fought hard enough for it—until he didn't want it any more.

He picked up the pace, going deeper, taking more. He wanted all of her. All her pleasure, all her desire, all her passion. Her moans turned to frantic sobs as she clung to his shoulders. Her nails raked over the slight scar from the wound she'd caused, but he welcomed the sting as he held onto the edge and ruthlessly worked the spot he knew would drive her wild.

The madness—to own her, to possess her—overtook him as the climax gripped the base of his spine. She massaged his length, the spasms of her second orgasm forcing him over the edge. The titanic climax exploded along his nerve-endings as he buried himself deep one last time and let himself tumble.

But as he rolled off her, his body shaky, his mind dazed from the intensity of the orgasm, he could hear the cry of that forgotten child clearly inside his head begging...

Don't leave me.

Before he managed to smother it again.

CHAPTER ELEVEN

KASIA TREMBLED, feeling dazed and disorientated and exposed as she watched Raif stand up.

He didn't speak to her, didn't even look at her, as he strolled to the door of the bathroom then disappeared inside. She heard the toilet flush, could see his reflection in the wall of mirrors as he washed his hands, having discarded the condom.

The sudden rush of insecurity she'd thought she had conquered a lifetime ago made her shiver.

Maybe you are not as unlike your mother as you want to believe?

How could she have given in to the rampant desire—again—when so much between them was in turmoil?

Not so much. *Everything.* Everything between them was in turmoil.

He hadn't wanted her apology for the wound she had caused—and genuinely didn't appear to blame her for all the pain and suffering he had endured after his ride to follow her, even though she was finding it hard not to blame herself—and he hadn't repeated his demand that they marry.

But what would happen when she told him about the pregnancy?

He wasn't the same man he had been when she'd left Narabia five and a half years ago. In many ways this man was even more of a stranger than the man to whom she'd given her virginity.

Why hadn't he told her about the drastic change in his circumstances while they were in the desert? She sat up and wrapped the bed sheet around her naked body, taking in the luxury suite, the magnificent views of London's landmarks across the Thames.

She lifted her dress off the floor with shaking fingers. She really ought to leave. She needed more time to consider how she was going to break the news to Raif about his impending fatherhood and shore up her own defences.

'What are you doing?'

She whipped around, her dress slipping through her fingers. He stood silhouetted in the bathroom doorway, his broad shoulders cutting out the light, completely unconcerned by his nakedness. She noticed the livid scar above his right hip from the emergency operation he had required and shuddered.

'I thought I should go,' she said, wanting to sound adamant but strangely conflicted about her course of action.

'Don't.' His bare feet padded on the carpet as he crossed the room. He sat on the edge of the bed. 'I don't want you to,' he added, as he curled his fingers around her neck and tugged her closer.

Her choice wasn't about what he wanted. But when he placed a kiss on her temple, the tenderness of the gesture was so compelling her resolve faltered.

'Stay with me tonight,' he said, running his thumb over her cheekbone, his watchful gaze so intent on her reaction she felt it echo at her core.

His sensual lips quirked in an assured smile. 'We left a lot unfinished. I think you agree.'

The heat climbed from her core into her cheeks. How did he do that? How did he read her responses so easily? But before she had a chance to feel embarrassed or, worse, threatened by how gauche she must appear to him, his gaze drifted to her hair.

'Your hair is lopsided,' he said.

She pressed a hand to the up-do and discovered it had tumbled down on one side.

'I should… I should really go,' she said, but as she attempted to scoot backwards off the bed, he captured her wrist and halted her getaway.

'No, you shouldn't,' he said. 'Let me help. It must be uncomfortable,' he added. It wasn't really, but as he proceeded to locate the pins holding her hair aloft, pluck them out and throw them away, her heart began to pummel her ribcage.

She watched him as he concentrated on the task, the care he was taking making her heart melt.

'How did you tame it?' he asked with a frown—as if he preferred it wild.

'A curling iron,' she said, her breathing catching again.

'An iron! Does that not hurt?' he said, his frown becoming concerned.

Her heart rate jumped, but still she smiled. 'No.'

He sank his fingers into the mass of curls she'd spent an hour arranging that afternoon as she'd practised the speech she'd never had a chance to give him. A moan escaped as he massaged her scalp, lifting and dividing the heavy weight.

She shivered, the delicious sensation rippling through her and reawakening the heat at her core that she'd thought would be sated for ever only minutes before.

'It feels good?' he asked.

'Yes, very good.'

Too good.

She didn't want to go now, she wanted to stay. But could she risk it?

'Turn around,' he said, and she did as he'd commanded.

He tugged on the sheet she had wrapped around her torso and she tightened her grip, but he only chuckled. 'Let it go, you do not need it. I promise not to ravage you again until you ask.'

She let the sheet fall, but crossed her arms over her naked breasts, brutally aware of her reflection in the window.

She sat on the bed naked, his large silhouette behind her as his thumbs dug into the tight muscles of her neck. She had to bite off another groan as his fingers worked their magic, finding each knot and releasing it, melting her resistance as they went.

At last he reached her bottom and the moan escaped.

He gave her butt a playful slap. 'Stop that, or I will not be responsible for my actions.'

Her eyes flew open. She met his gaze in the glass. He was smiling, but his jaw was tense. And she could feel his erection against her back.

She swung around, not as wary as she had been.

She would tell him about the baby soon. But there was no reason to tell him tonight. Would it be so wrong to enjoy this time with him, while he was relaxed—or more relaxed than usual—and playful?

Reaching out, he ran his thumb under her nipple and made her gasp. She felt it squeeze and tighten, instantly responsive to his touch.

'It is strange, but they seem larger than I remember them,' he said.

Because they were.

She thanked God for the shadows in the room so he couldn't read the guilty look that crossed her face. He dipped his head, ready to take the aching peak into his mouth and build the hunger again, but she drew back.

'Is something wrong?' he asked, instantly alert to her hesitation.

Her heart pounded hard. How could this man be so aware of her needs, her wants?

'Could we...? Is it okay if we just talk for a minute?'

His eyebrows rose. 'This is not what a man in my state likes to hear,' he said boldly, but his lips had quirked in a strained half-smile and she knew he was joking. Or mostly joking.

Climbing off the bed, he found the boxer briefs he had discarded earlier and put them on, then walked to the bathroom and returned with a fluffy robe. 'You had better put this on.' He threw the robe to her and she stuffed her arms into it, wrapped the belt around and tied it.

He had picked up the phone next to the bed-side. 'Are you hungry?'

She nodded. The truth was she was ravenous, and for much more than food. He looked ridiculously gorgeous standing there in his boxer shorts, but she wanted to speak to him and food felt like the perfect distraction. Also, she hadn't eaten since before she'd done the test that morning, thanks to her nerves.

'Is there anything you don't eat?' he asked.

'Sheep's eyeballs,' she said, knowing it was a delicacy of the Kholadi, and he laughed at her joke.

'You do not know what you are missing,' he

said, then reeled a selection of delicious items off the room-service menu.

Her stomach rumbled as he sat on the bed, leaning against the headboard. Stretching out his legs, he beckoned her. 'Come.'

She crawled towards him, impossibly touched when he wrapped an arm around her. She went to rest against his right side, enjoying the moment of closeness, but remembered the appendectomy scar just in time.

'I'm sorry.'

'Stop apologising,' he said, tugging her back down again, until she was nestled under his arm. 'It doesn't hurt.'

She didn't entirely believe him, but he seemed unconcerned. He was clearly a man who had endured a lot of pain in his life—enough that a wound such as this was insignificant.

'What is it you wish to talk about?' he asked.

There were so, so many things she wanted to know about him, she realised, but she didn't have the right to ask them. Not until she had told him about her baby. Their baby. So she settled for something she did have the right to know.

'Why did you pretend you were still just the

Kholadi Chief at the oasis...' *Just.* The qualifier echoed in her consciousness.

Whatever had happened to change his circumstances in the last five years, to turn him into a billionaire with considerable power and influence outside his desert kingdom, he had never been *just* a chieftain. He had always been charming, intelligent, a brilliant political strategist and a worthy diplomatic opponent, according to Zane. Hadn't Cat once mentioned that he spoke seven languages fluently?

The Bad-Boy Sheikh tag was one the girls in the palace's women's quarters had created for him, because it had added to the fantasies they'd all whispered about him. It had made him hotter. But he really didn't need to be any hotter than he already was. Maybe he had no formal education, unlike her, but he had risen to the task of leading his people as a teenager and she would guess that was the motive behind what he was doing here now.

She looked up at him. His brows quirked, the smile widening, and she wondered why her question amused him.

'I did not pretend to be something I am not.'

'But you could have told me about your other

life. Your life in the West. As a businessman. Why didn't you?' She looked away, out into the night sky. Embarrassed at the memory of telling him about Cambridge University as if he would never have heard of the place.

Wow, she'd really messed up—in so many ways.

Strong fingers captured her chin and tugged her gaze to his. The sparkle of amusement had died, his eyes intent. 'You think because I have money now, because I know how to work the stock market, how to invest and diversify the riches of my people, my country, so they can have more options, that this makes me a better man than I was before?'

She shook her head furiously. 'No, no, not at all.' She had insulted him and it hadn't been her intention. 'But it does make you different from the man I believed you to be.'

'How?' he said. 'I am the same man underneath the suit as the robe. As you can see.' He spread his arm out, drawing her eyes to the many scars on his chest, illuminated by the light from the bathroom, the red marks where her nails had scored his skin during their lovemaking, and the faded ink of the tattoo. 'It is only your perception that is different.'

Was it? Perhaps he was right, and her impression of him was about her own prejudices—her own fantasies. And the truth was that so much of him was unchanged from their night in the desert. But, still, she couldn't quite give up her argument.

'Really? Would you have chosen to get that tattoo now?' she asked, seizing on the crude, pagan and unsettling design—which made him look even more wild than all the injuries he had suffered. He must have got it when he'd become Chief of the Kholadi, as a teenager, the serpent a well-known symbol of the tribe.

He glanced at his shoulder, almost as if he had forgotten the tattoo was there. Then stared back at her.

'This tattoo was not my choice. My father had me inked before he threw me out.'

'Sheikh Tariq forced you to have that tattoo?' Shock and sympathy hit her like a punch to the stomach. 'But… Why?'

'So everyone would know I was nothing more than a Kholadi whore's brat.'

She tried to absorb the horror of that, and the

sadness at the casual way he made the remark. 'How old were you?'

He shrugged, making the snake writhe in the dim light. 'Ten.'

Ten? 'But that's… That's hideous.'

She'd heard the stories about Tariq's abuse of Zane. When she and Cat had gone to the marketplace together during the early days of her friend's employment, an old woman who had delivered fabric to the palace had told of how Zane had been beaten for trying to run away, after being kidnapped from his mother in LA.

Why was she even surprised that Tariq had treated his other son with equal brutality? The old Sheikh had become mad with bitterness after Zelda Mayhew, Zane's mother, had run away from him with her baby son. But this wasn't just cruel, it was twisted. To permanently mark a child, to treat him with such contempt, your own flesh and blood. How could Tariq have done such a thing? And how had Raif survived it?

'Do not be distressed.' He sent her a confused half-smile. 'I survived. Once you get used to the needle, it doesn't hurt. And I wear the tattoo with pride now as the Kholadi's Chief. He was crueller to my mother.'

* * *

The minute he had mentioned his mother, Raif knew he should not have done. Because Kasia shot upright, dislodging his arm, the curiosity in her gaze outstripped by the concern and compassion that had already turned her eyes into twin pools of amber. Pools he had lost himself in a moment ago.

Was that why he'd mentioned his mother, because he was basking in the compassion? Exactly how weak and pathetic did that make him?

'Your mother? You mean…' She paused and looked down, her fingers toying with the robe's belt. She didn't want to say the word, he realised—and was trying to think of a more polite way to describe her. At last she raised her chin, the honest sympathy turning the pang in his chest to an ache.

'I'm sorry, I only know the stories about your mother, that she was a…' He waited for her to say it, a word he had heard many times, a word he himself had used to describe his mother. A word he had always been determined to own. People had judged him because of her and he had hated her for it, but had refused to admit the shame he felt, persuading anyone who would listen, his brother included, that he was proud to be a whore's son.

Strange to realise that when he'd finally discovered the truth about her, two years ago, while reading his father's papers, the only real emotion he had felt, instead of anger or regret or sadness for the woman who had given birth to a sheikh's son and been destroyed in the process, had been a vague feeling of disappointment. That he had gone through his childhood, his whole adult life fighting to prove it didn't matter that his mother was something she had never really been.

'That she was Tariq's paid companion,' Kasia finally managed.

The ache in his chest became more pronounced when he realised how hard Kasia was trying to spare his feelings. Feelings that no longer existed. Or hadn't until he'd taken her virginity all those weeks ago and triggered a reaction he'd found hard to explain.

'A whore, you mean?' he said flatly.

'I wouldn't use that term,' Kasia replied fiercely.

'Why not, if it is the truth?' He was baiting her now, and he knew it, because the truth about his mother was more complex. But he couldn't help wondering how Kasia would have reacted to his heritage if his mother had been the whore everyone had convinced him she was? Would Kasia have judged him, too? And his mother? Or was her sweetness, her innocence as real as it appeared?

'Because it's a cruel and derogatory term and it doesn't take into account why women are often forced to make those choices,' she said without hesitation, the passionate defence making the ache in his chest worse.

Apparently she was as sweet as she appeared.

He wondered how different his life might have been if he had met Kasia before the lies about his birth—and the degradation he had suffered because of them—had forced him to grow up far too soon and had hardened him into the cynic he was today? He rubbed his knuckles over his chest, determined to take the foolish ache away. They could not turn back the clock. Maybe he had become the man he was today—hard, cynical, immune to love—based on a lie, but he had no desire to change who he was.

'Perhaps it is good, then, she was not so much of a whore after all,' he said, deciding to tell

Kasia the truth. 'Or not until after she became pregnant with me.'

'I don't… I don't understand,' she said. 'But I thought she died when you were born?'

'She did,' he said, then watched her make the connection. His mother had taken men into her bed for money while she had been with child.

A part of him wanted to let Kasia believe that was all there was to the story, the truth he had lived with his entire life. What difference did it really make *why* his mother had become a prostitute? And when?

But instead of looking shocked, or disgusted, Kasia's eyes brimmed with tears and the ache he was trying to numb started to pulse again.

'Why are you crying?' he said, as he watched her swipe the moisture away.

'She must have been so desperate. I can't even imagine it.'

No one had ever cried for his mother, no one had ever mourned her, not even him. But as he watched a single tear track down Kasia's cheek, something was released inside him and the prickle of guilt and shame—in himself, not his mother—that he had held at bay joined the brutal ache in his chest.

Why would she cry for his mother? Defend her? Lament the terrible choices his mother had been forced to make?

And if this girl could cry for her, who had never known her, and still only knew the worst about her, how much of a bastard did it make him that he could not?

'She *was* desperate,' he said, no longer able to deny the truth he had never confided in anyone, never wanted to acknowledge or confront, until now. 'She was a virgin, only sixteen years old when he took her to his bed. But he refused to marry her, and when she became pregnant he discarded her, had her branded a whore. She did not return to the Kholadi because of the shame, so she ended up in a brothel in Zafari,' he said, mentioning the city that had sprawled around the walls of the Golden Palace for generations.

'The madam there brought me to the palace after my mother died in childbirth. And the women took me in. My father was furious, of course, but even he could not order a baby cast out of the palace, especially one that carried his blood, however tainted. But he never acknowledged me and always refused to see me—until Zane arrived in the palace and Tariq wanted me gone. Everyone told me always that my mother was a whore, and I believed it, but I found out two years ago, when Zane gave me our father's journals, that it was not the whole truth.'

He had been furious with Zane for giving the journals to him and insisting he read them, especially when he had discovered the inconvenient truth contained within them. He had felt nothing for his mother's plight, his heart already hardened towards her, but he had been instantly suspicious of Zane's motives.

Why would Zane presume he would want to unearth ancient history? To revisit something about his birth that would rewrite the principles on which he had founded his life? Was Zane expecting him to be grateful? Expecting him to give Narabia political and economic concessions in their trade negotiations in gratitude for this interference in his private life? Or was it even simpler than that? Did Zane simply wish to weaken him?

Zane, of all people, had to know that the chaos, the struggles, the disadvantages of his childhood had ultimately given him strength—therefore he must have known that showing Raif that his mother had been a victim too might undermine that strength.

But as Raif watched Kasia struggle to hold back her tears, the sympathy and understanding in her eyes probed that place deep inside him that he had never wanted anyone to find—and the ache in his chest rose up to push against his larynx.

No. No. No.

Kasia pressed a hand to her belly, trying to contain the pain, not just at the hideous truths Raif had revealed about his childhood and his mother's mistreatment and exploitation but also at the guilt tying her stomach in tight knots. Because Raif's revelations about his mother put a whole new complexion on what had happened a month ago.

'Is that why...?' She paused, her throat dry as the guilt sharpened. 'Is that why you were so insistent we marry? Why you wanted to obey the Law of Marriage of the Sheikhs.'

Had he been trying to right the wrongs his father had done his mother, and him, by observing the same sacred law his father had broken so callously?

She had so easily dismissed his demand that they marry as a backward and autocratic request based on arrogance and a misguided honour system that had no place in modern society, but it had always been much more personal than that. How could it not be after what he had discovered about his mother's treatment? She had put him in an untenable position by not telling him about her virginity, then had compounded it by dismissing his attempt to solve the problem. She had used him for her own pleasure, and then underestimated him at every turn.

'I don't know.' He shrugged, the movement stiff. 'I'm not sure what I was thinking at the time. I was shocked by your untouched state. I had not expected it. Or the intensity of our lovemaking.'

Her skin flushed at the bald statement, and the knots in her abdomen heated. She wasn't sure whether she was moved or flattered or simply aroused by his honesty and the knowledge she wasn't the only one who had been blindsided by their intense physical connection.

'But afterwards…' He sighed. 'Especially as I lay for days in the Golden Palace with nothing to do, I kept recalling our last moments together.

And questioning why I had been so inflexible, so belligerent, so determined to insist upon marriage.' He hesitated. 'And it occurred to me that maybe I was more affected by what I had learned about my parents' past than I had assumed.'

'I'm so sorry,' she said. 'For putting you in that position.' It wasn't the first time she had apologised for not telling him of her virginity, but it was the first time she had meant it without reservation.

Maybe she'd had no knowledge of his past, his priorities, when she had slept with him, but she had assumed he was a thoughtless man, and had never examined his motives properly. His honour was important to him, not because he was arrogant or overbearing but because he had been forced to fight for it every single day of his life.

He lifted her hand, stared at her fingers as he brushed his thumb across her knuckles.

The heat in her stomach warmed further and glowed, and seemed to wrap itself around her heart, making her ribs feel tight.

The guilt twisted, though, when he raised his head, his expression tense. And guarded.

'I think perhaps it is *I* who should apologise to *you*,' he said, his voice gruff but forceful.

'Why?' she asked.

He touched a finger to her cheek, drew a tendril of hair behind her ear. Then sent her a lopsided smile that made her heartbeat slow and thicken.

'For trying to bully you into marriage, perhaps?' he murmured, the rueful twist of his lips beguiling. 'And for scaring you away. If I had not reacted so recklessly, made such a ridiculous demand, we could have found a better way to end our time at the oasis, is this not so?'

She forced a smile to her lips, stifling the ripple of sadness that he now considered marriage a 'ridiculous demand'. Of course he did, because it *was* ridiculous, they didn't know each other. Not really.

Should she tell him now, about the baby? The question had the guilt tightening in her stomach, but she dismissed it. Why destroy this moment of closeness, of connection? She would tell him soon, just not yet.

At least now she knew she didn't have to be scared to tell him when the time came. He was a much more intelligent and thoughtful man than she had given him credit for, despite the harshness of his upbringing.

'Perhaps we both need to apologise?' she offered.

He chuckled, the sound helping to release the knot of guilt still lodged in her belly. 'An excellent compromise.'

Warmth flooded her system at the approval in his gaze.

She would tell him about the pregnancy soon, but for tonight she just wanted to enjoy his company.

He was the father of her child, and while this liaison was based on a sexual connection and would not last—because they were still such different people, with such different goals in life— he would always have a place in her life now. And her child's life. It was good to know that didn't scare her any more, it excited her. She hadn't given much thought to what kind of father he would make, had been too scared to consider it because of her assumptions about the kind of man he was—rough, uneducated, wild—but now she could see she didn't need to be scared about that either.

He cradled her face, pulled her close for a kiss, and the pheromones gathered—as they always did—to overwhelm her thoughts. But as his lips touched hers, the electric contact sending a familiar shiver down her spine, a loud knock sounded in the next room.

'Mr Khan, room service. We have your order.'

He swore against her lips in Kholadi—his frustration palpable—and she let out a strained laugh.

Shifting to kiss her forehead, he drew back. 'I think we had better let them in,' he said, not sounding at all pleased at the prospect.

'Must we?' she shot back, surprising herself. Was she actually pouting?

He let out a rough chuckle. 'Unfortunately, yes, my little witch.'

The hot promise in his eyes had the heat rushing straight to her core as he climbed off the bed.

'You need to build up your stamina for the night ahead,' he added, wiggling his brows as he teased her.

The flush exploded in her core as she watched him stride across the bedroom in his boxer briefs. Her gaze drifted down the line of his spine and snagged on the bunch of muscle in his taut backside.

She would tell him about the baby soon, but for tonight she wanted to indulge in the pleasure of having him all to herself. And make full use of the chance to get to know him better. A *lot* better.

She choked off a playful laugh.

In every possible sense of the word!

CHAPTER TWELVE

KASIA AWOKE THE next morning feeling warm and sated and a little overwhelmed by the feel of Raif's big body wrapped around hers. His arm was draped over her waist, his even breathing stroked her nape. His hard chest pressed against her back, his muscular thighs cradled her own legs and something long and firm nestled against her bottom.

She blinked, adjusting to the morning light flooding through the open curtains, and couldn't stop a grin from spreading across her face.

Who would have guessed the Bad-Boy Sheikh was a secret snuggler?

But, then, there were so many things she'd discovered about him last night. Information that she'd stored away carefully to take out and examine at a later date. Not just the devastating details about his childhood but also what she'd learned about his strength of character, his code of honour and his ability to admit when he was wrong.

The heat settled in her abdomen, loosening her thigh muscles and making her feel giddy at the memory of all the times he'd taken her during the night. That first time, fast and furious and frantic, and unbearably exciting.

And then later, as they'd sat eating together and he'd insisted on feeding her a bite of his steak, the succulent flavour had exploded on her tongue and she'd groaned. The food had been abandoned, and they'd ended up back in the bedroom—and this time the fire had built slowly, sensuously. He'd made her beg, using his tongue and teeth and touch to drive her insane. Around midnight, they'd bathed together in the whirlpool tub in the suite's bathroom and then started all over again, making the delicious discovery that she could drive him insane in return. She'd finally dropped into a deep, dreamless sleep with his arms around her.

She sighed, the surge of arousal nothing new, but in the stark light of morning came self-consciousness as well.

Shifting on the bed, she lifted his arm and scooted out from under it. Laying it down again, she heard him grunt. He had rolled over onto his back.

She had to cover her mouth to hold in her delighted laugh at the sight of his beautiful torso, all strong lines and sculpted contours, revealed by the sheet lying low on his hips and the tent formed by his morning erection.

Liquid heat throbbed at her core.

Yes, she would definitely have to take care of that erection soon, but first things first. She needed to wash her face, check her hair hadn't gone completely wild during the night, brush her teeth and work out the etiquette for the morning after a night such as the one they had just shared. She could feel delicious tenderness in her sex, the rub of beard burn on her nipples. Was that normal?

She tiptoed across the room, plucked the bathrobe off the floor where it had been flung during their mad dash back to bed after supper, and put it on. But as she walked passed the open door to the living area, a vague whiff of last night's dinner hit her nostrils.

Nausea rose from nowhere like a tidal wave. Slamming a hand over her mouth, she dashed into the bathroom, reaching the toilet just in time before her stomach and everything inside it heaved.

When the violent retching finally stopped, she flushed away the evidence of her first bout of morning sickness and slid into a sitting position on the floor. Exhausted.

The nausea still sat like a crouching tiger under her breastbone, ready to pounce, the subtle scent of rose perfume from the vanity offending her nostrils.

She gulped in air. But as she gripped the vanity unit, attempting to hold the new wave of nausea at bay, a deep voice—thick with concern—had her jerking round.

'Kasia, what's wrong? Have you just vomited?'

Panic gripped her already tender insides as Raif crossed the room. He wore only the boxer briefs, but the jolt of arousal that always accompanied the glorious sight of his nearly naked body was short-lived.

Her stomach rebelled.

He grabbed her, holding her upright on unsteady legs and sweeping the wild hair back from her face as she bent over the toilet.

'I've got you,' he said, stroking her back as she retched. The wave finally passed as her stomach emptied, leaving her exhausted and shaky. And terrified.

Tears leaked from her eyes, emotion and anxiety overwhelming her.

Why did the sickness have to hit for the first time this morning?

She'd felt vaguely queasy in the last week, but she'd hadn't been prepared for anything like this. And the last thing she wanted was for him to witness it.

'Has it passed?' he asked gently.

She nodded. 'Yes, I think so.'

Dropping the toilet seat, he directed her to sit on it, then filled a glass with water.

She had to leave. She needed more time to work out the best possible way to break the news of her pregnancy to him. And having to admit it while she was sitting on the toilet of his luxury bathroom, with her hair rioting around her head as if she'd been electrocuted and her nipples still sore from his lovemaking, definitely wasn't that moment.

The anxiety she'd taken a break from the night before bounced back.

She didn't feel sexy and empowered any more. She felt weak, inadequate and worn out.

'Sip this,' he said, handing her the glass. She did as she was told, but the cool, refreshing liquid soothing her raw throat did nothing to tame the anxiety still churning in her stomach as she watched him rip Cellophane off a new toothbrush then add toothpaste, and run it under the tap.

Taking the glass from her, he handed her the prepared toothbrush.

She brushed her teeth, aware of his watchful gaze.

'What do you think has caused this sickness?' he asked when she had finished rinsing out her mouth.

She concentrated on wiping her lips, deliberately avoiding eye contact as she spoke. 'It must have been something I ate.'

But even she could hear the tremble of dishonesty in her voice. She had always been a terrible liar.

'I should probably head home,' she said, more firmly. 'It might be a bug and I don't want you to catch it, too.'

He hadn't said anything, hadn't even moved.

She swallowed down the lump of shame at her deception. She couldn't deal with him now, not in this condition.

If she could just get out of here, she would be

able to regroup, recharge, re-evaluate. At least her stomach had finally settled.

But as she dropped the towel on the vanity and turned to go, his fingers closed around her biceps. 'Not so fast. Look at me, Kasia.' He grasped her chin.

Their gazes connected and the guilt exploded in her chest like a nuclear bomb as he studied her face, the mushroom cloud billowing across her collarbone and rising into her cheeks.

'We ate the same thing, and I am not sick,' he said, but she could hear it already in his voice—the edge of suspicion. And see it in the hooded look in his dark eyes. 'And if it was a stomach bug, I doubt it would have resolved itself so quickly.'

'Please, I have to go.' She tried to wrestle her arm free, the frantic urge to flee overcoming her, even though a part of her knew it was already too late.

Raif was not a stupid man, and he could read her far too easily.

His grip on her arm tightened, a muscle in his jaw flexing as his gaze dipped to take in the swell of her cleavage. And assess the size of her breasts again, which he had noticed the night before were larger than they had been. When his gaze returned to hers, the last of the warmth and concern had leached away, to be replaced by the brutal chill of anger.

Guilt and regret combined in the pit of her stomach to create a deep well of sadness.

The guarded, wary cynicism in his eyes, which had been banished the night before—as they'd eaten and talked and bathed together, as they had made love—had returned.

The closeness, the connection was gone so quickly she wondered if it had ever really existed in the first place, especially when he spoke again, the bite of contempt evident in every syllable:

'Answer me without lying this time, are you carrying my child?'

Raif could see the answer in her face before she replied.

'Yes,' she said, then ducked her head.

The slow-burning fury in his gut turned to white-hot rage but worse than that was the stabbing pain of her betrayal.

Kasia carried his child and she had not told him. Had she ever intended to tell him?

She had said nothing all through the night they had spent together. While he had taken her with fire, with passion more times than he could count. But also while they had talked, and communicated with more than words.

When he had woken up a few minutes ago, the first thing he had done was reach for her. The wave of panic when he had found her gone had been real and devastating and not just because of the painful erection he'd been sporting. He hadn't just wanted to take her again, he had wanted to hold her, to touch her, to capture her in his arms and keep her with him. He had never had that need for any other human being in his entire life. He had tried to dismiss it, forced himself to control it, but that instant visceral yearning had scared him on a fundamental level.

The sound of her in the bathroom had brought with it a wave of relief, which had only disturbed him more.

As he had stared at the ornate plasterwork on the ceiling, willing his erection to subside—not easy while her scent filled his nostrils—he had forced himself to assess all they had done the night before, and had tried to figure out what had happened to him.

Kasia had captivated and aroused him, intoxicated him with her passion, her wildfire responses, yes, but more than that he had found a closeness with her during the hours they had spent together. As they had talked, as they had teased each other.

He had spoken of things in his life he had never told another living soul. Not just the truth about his mother, but the truth about the tattoo—how his father had him branded like cattle. The more he'd thought about everything he had said and done, the weaker he'd felt.

Why had he trusted her? When he had never truly trusted anyone in his life? And after so short an acquaintance?

But then his hearing had tuned into the noise from the bathroom and he'd realised she was being sick. All he'd wanted to do was help her.

She'd looked so fragile, seemed so shaky in his arms. He'd held her while she'd retched and felt wretched himself.

That, too, had been a brand-new sensation. If he had been in a similar situation before, not that he ever had, his inclination would have been to allow his lover her privacy. But with Kasia, as with everything else about them, he had been determined to intervene.

Had he sensed her condition the night before? Was that why he had felt this weird connection to her? Had revealed information that he had never trusted anyone to know before now?

It had to be, he thought, desperate to dismiss the hollow feeling that had started to seep into his bones.

She had betrayed him. Had hidden the truth from him. And that he could never forgive.

'Why did you not tell me?' he asked, struggling to control the rage, not just at her deception but at his own stupidity.

Her face lifted. The sheen of tears looked genuine, but he steeled himself against them.

She had deceived him, deliberately. The tears weren't real.

'I wanted to wait for the right time,' she said, her voice faltering. She dropped her chin, to stare at the fingers she was clutching. 'Last night was…' Her jaw clenched. 'Last night was special, I didn't want to ruin it.'

His heart swelled, but he pushed his fury to the fore.

She had deceived him and manipulated him

into telling her things he should never have revealed. He would not make that mistake again.

He could not undo last night—but he could use it to his advantage, something he was more than prepared to do for the sake of his child.

His gaze dropped, to take in the swell of her breasts where the lapels of her robe drooped. The surge of heat was inevitable and familiar—and gloriously uncomplicated—the surge of possessiveness not so much. But still it made sense. His child grew inside her. He had always known he would have to become a father, that he would need to have heirs to ensure a peaceful transition of power within his tribe.

Yes, there was his honour to be considered too now. The urge to protect his honour at the oasis, which had made him demand marriage, an urge he had been determined to dismiss only last night as a knee-jerk reaction to the circumstances of his birth, had become stronger than ever.

He needed to start thinking clearly again. Thinking pragmatically. And make decisions based on the good of his people, his position, not based on weakness or want or the whims of a girl he couldn't even trust.

The child was the only thing that mattered now… His child and the child he had once been. He would give this child the legacy he had worked for twenty years to create, ever since a small band of Kholadi tribesman had discovered him abandoned and dying in the desert, his shoulder covered in scabs from the enforced tattoo, and had recognised him as one of their own.

He owed his tribe his loyalty and his life. He owed this girl neither.

Tucking a finger under her chin, he lifted her gaze back to his and forced himself to hold onto his fury. And ignored the shiver of sensation that always assailed him when he touched her. This indiscriminate desire would come in useful in the years ahead. But for now he had to ask the only question that mattered.

'Do you intend to keep the child?'

'Yes,' she said, covering her belly with her clasped hands as if to instinctively protect the babe within from the suggestion of termination.

He nodded, resenting the leap in his chest.

It was not joy or gratitude he felt. Why should he be grateful or joyous when she had chosen to keep the very existence of this child from him?

'Then we must be married as soon as possible.'

'No!' She stepped back, her eyebrows shooting up as if she was surprised by his demand, panic sparking in her eyes. 'That's not... I can't marry you.'

He grasped her arm, the fear that she would run again churning in his gut, but he clung onto his fury, forced himself to loosen his grip. She still appeared fragile and shaky from the bout of nausea. And bullying her had not worked before. Which meant he would have to reason with her. Something that would be a great deal easier if her nearness didn't fire every one of his senses, and her refusal to accept their situation didn't make his temper ignite.

'There is no other option now,' he said, struggling to bite down not just on his fury but also his resentment. 'I will not have my child born a bastard, as I was.' He ground out the words, hating that he was being forced to reveal his feelings again, feelings he wished he had never shared. 'As the mother of my child, you will become my princess, you will have everything you could ever want, and our child will be heir to the Kholadi principality. Is that not enough?' He was offering her everything he had. How dared she refuse him?

'No.' She tugged her arm loose. 'Because I won't have the one thing I want most. A choice.'

It was the same argument she had used before, the argument that he had eventually agreed to last night, after much soul-searching. But the situation was very different now. They weren't independent people any more. They were parents and they must protect their child.

'There are no choices now,' he said. 'Not for either of us.'

'I refuse to believe that, there is *always* a choice,' she said, the tears spilling over her lids.

These tears were not fake, even he was forced to acknowledge as much despite his resentment.

Her wariness and her regret were replaced by pride and stubbornness in the upward tilt of her chin and the stiff set of her shoulders. She was prepared to fight him on this, and there was something about her bravery and determination that had a tiny kernel of respect blossoming inside him. But he refused to give in to it.

He had given way once before. He would not do so again.

'The only choice now is marriage,' he said.

'I can't marry without love,' she said, as she straightened. 'And I won't.'

'*Love!*' The enraged shout came out before he could think better of it. 'There is no such thing as love. It is romantic *nonsense*. If that is what you have learned from your fancy education, it is better you stop wasting my brother's money.'

He had gone too far, said too much, even though every word was true. Her body went rigid, the fierce compassion sparking in her eyes that had stirred him to make so many reckless, foolish decisions from the moment he'd met her.

'That you think love is nonsense is precisely why I would never choose to marry *you*.' She hurled the words at him, the fire and passion reverberating through her slender body, then turned and fled from the room.

He swore viciously in Kholadi, the ugly curses echoing off the marble surfaces like rifle shots.

He forced himself to breathe, waiting for the squeezing pain in his lungs to ease, and stayed rooted to the spot, even though his instinct was to storm after her. Not to let her get away.

He curled his fingers into fists, clenched his teeth so tight he was surprised his jaw didn't crack, and waited for the storm of destructive, counter-productive emotions to pass. Or pass enough for him to think clearly.

He knew how to conduct a negotiation. But he had blown this one, by letting her see how much he wanted this marriage. He had shown his hand too early and then allowed his frustration, his need to distract him from his goals.

They *would* be married. That much was non-negotiable. But bullying her and shouting at her was not the answer. It was how his father had always behaved. And it made him less of a man.

He could hear her getting dressed in the bedroom. A part of him, a very large part of him, wanted to stalk in there and stop her from leaving. As he was sure she intended to do—because running away was her default.

But instead of doing so, he stalked to the sink and turned on the tap.

He washed his hands and face, threw cold water on his chest, to contain the anger—and the passion still rioting through his body and evident not just in the pounding pain in his head but the stiff column of flesh stretching his boxers.

When he had finally calmed himself enough to control the fury, the passion and the pain, he walked out of the bathroom.

The bedroom was empty, as he had suspected it might be. A scrawled note lay on the bed, propped on the unkempt sheets where they had devoured each other during the night. He picked it up. As he read the note, some of the writing smudged with what had to be her tears, the fury and frustration twisted his gut again.

I'm sorry I didn't tell you about the baby last night. That was wrong of me. And I apologise.

But the reason I didn't was that I feared exactly this reaction from you. We cannot be wed. Because love means everything to me and nothing to you. I want this child very much and I love it already. Rest assured it will never be a bastard to me.

Once it is born, we can speak again.

Until then, please don't contact me.

Kasia

He crushed the note in his fist. He would contact her again, and soon. She could not run far this time, only to the college he already had the power to control with the funding he had offered.

He refused to give up on the necessity of marriage, as he had far too easily before, because much more than just his honour was at stake now.

His child grew inside her. That gave him rights

and responsibilities he could not shirk. Rights and responsibilities he *would* not shirk.

He could not allow his child to be born defenceless, without his name, his wealth and the legacy he had fought so hard to create. But neither would he turn into his father to get what he wanted.

So he must figure out a strategy to force Kasia to see what was right in front of her eyes.

No child deserved to be born without its father's name, its father's protection.

Love was not enough. It couldn't feed you or clothe you, it couldn't fight your enemies for you or shelter you from a storm.

He could not change her fanciful, foolishly romantic notions, but she was smart and intuitive and she wanted him—as much as he wanted her—so he would find a way to persuade her that marriage was the only option.

If that meant charming her, bribing her, seducing her, blackmailing her or even kidnapping her, dammit. He would do it. He could not fail.

Because the one thing he would never do was abandon his child.

CHAPTER THIRTEEN

Ms Salah, please come to my office immediately.

KASIA STARED AT the text from Dean Walmsley. The dropping sensation in her already oversensitive stomach exacerbated the tangle of anxiety.

She took a sip of her tea and a tentative nibble of the dry crackers she had been advised to snack on by her doctor, then gathered up her backpack and the textbooks she was returning to the library.

She would speak to Dean Walmsley on the way.

She had been expecting this confrontation for over a week, ever since she had returned from London. All she could do now was pray that he hadn't been informed of the full extent of her unprofessionalism at the funding event. He'd been furious when he'd called her to his office on the

Monday morning to inform her that Alice Evershot had emailed him to say the funding had not been forthcoming from the donor she had met.

Given that the donor was Raif, she was not remotely surprised at the decision to withdraw the offer. That she would have to wait to hear if she would receive the funding she needed for her PhD seemed somehow fitting in the circumstances as payback for the mistakes she'd made. She could not accept the funding from Raif now anyway, because it would give him a hold over her that could cause massive complications given their personal relationship.

Not that they had a personal relationship, she thought wearily as she made her way through the campus buildings towards Dean Walmsley's office. The only thing that connected them now was the baby.

She'd had no word from Raif in the last week, which she should have been glad about. He must have read her note, realised she would have made him a terrible consort and decided not to contact her again until after the baby was born.

So why was she so disappointed? She didn't want to have another confrontation with him on the question of marriage. But at the same time she couldn't ignore the deep well of sadness, the yearning in the last week every time she woke in her single bed after another night spent dreaming about him and missed that leaping joy when she had woken up on the Saturday morning to find his arms around her.

Perhaps it was simply that, despite their terrible row, she knew Raif, for all his cynicism about love, was not an insensitive man—*because* of the dreadful cruelties he had suffered as a child, not in spite of them.

Regret tightened her throat.

It's just the pregnancy hormones, Kaz, messing with you again. Even if you could have loved Raif, he could never have loved you back.

He had spent his whole life guarding against making himself vulnerable. And without vulnerability how could you have love? No matter how sensitive or intelligent he could be—the heat glowed in her stomach—or how attuned to he was to her sexual needs.

She trudged up the stairs of the red-brick building that housed the Dean's office.

It's a good thing he has seen reason—not a bad thing for you and your baby. Stop second-guessing yourself.

They would reach an accord together once the child was born, but to do that without enmity or anger, they needed a break now, which was precisely why she had asked that of him in her note. That he had respected her decision was a positive sign. He was not intractable, not averse to seeing reason.

She wanted very much for her son or daughter to know its father, to have a relationship with him and for him to have a relationship with his child. For that to happen, they needed to be able to negotiate with each other in good faith without the spectre of past hurts, past wrongs rearing their heads. To take time out was a good thing. That Raif had seen reason—and hadn't stalked straight after her—was therefore all good, even if it didn't feel that good at the moment.

Of course she felt vulnerable, scared, lonely. She was going to have to bring up her child alone. And find out how to continue her academic career as a single parent. She still hadn't gained the courage to contact Cat and tell her what was going on.

She blew out a breath as she reached the top of the stairs and headed down the corridor to

Walmsley's office and the bad news she was sure awaited her about her PhD.

If only she didn't feel so tired all the time—the bouts of nausea restricted themselves to the early morning, thank goodness—but the pregnancy, and the difficulty she'd had sleeping since she'd left Raif's bed, had also taken a heavy toll on her energy. Shifting the books in her arms, she tapped on the door to the Dean's office. 'Dean Walmsley, it's Kasia Salah.'

'Come in, Miss Salah,' came the curt response.

She straightened her spine, hearing the irritation in Walmsley's tone. Okay, that did not sound promising.

If the Dean was about to kick her out of the college, she would just have to find another way to get funding. The PhD she wanted to pursue was important to Narabia. And also important to her.

But the prickle of unease became an explosion as soon as she stepped into the office, and saw the man sitting in front of Walmsley's desk.

Raif.

He stood, his tall frame clad in a designer business suit silhouetted against the sunshine flooding through Walmsley's window.

'Miss Salah, it's about time you arrived. Mr Khan and I have been waiting…' Walmsley began to talk, but his reprimand was drowned out by the pounding in Kasia's ears.

Her gaze devoured Raif, the brutal awareness, the painful longing she couldn't seem to curtail or control only becoming more disturbing as she took in the flare of desire in his dark chocolate eyes and the harsh, unyielding line of his jaw.

The books in her arms clattered to the floor. But she couldn't seem to hear that either. All she could hear were the questions in her head peppering her like bullets as she tried to fight her misguided burst of joy at seeing him again.

Had he come here to demand marriage again? To bully her? To blackmail her? He was an extremely wealthy man—the college depended on donors like him to fund its postgraduate programme—which gave him a power over her career that she hadn't acknowledged until this moment.

'Miss Salah! What on earth is the matter with you?' Walmsley's horrified exclamation didn't really register either as she stumbled back, unable to take her eyes off Raif as he stepped towards her and bent to scoop up the books she'd dropped.

'What are you doing here?' she whispered as he straightened, his gaze locked on her face. The clean, intoxicating aroma of man and soap suffocated her.

'Mr Khan has come to talk more about the funding initiative,' Walmsley butted in. 'I have a lecture to give, so I will leave you two alone,' the Dean added with a sniff. 'Make sure you make a better impression this time, Miss Salah,' he finished, sending her a scathing look as he left the office.

But somehow she couldn't seem to engage with the Dean's censure as the door shut behind him, leaving her alone with Raif.

'Why are you really here?' she asked again, doubting the funding initiative had anything to do with Raif's presence in Cambridge.

'You know why, Kasia,' he said. 'Did you really believe I would abandon my child so easily?'

'I can't... I still can't marry you, Raif, my answer hasn't changed,' she said, feeling humiliated by the quiver in her voice.

He placed the books she had dropped on

Walmsley's desk without replying. Then, to her astonishment, he nodded.

'You do not wish to marry me, because you do not love me? Is this correct?'

It was the very last thing she had expected him to say. Of course, it wasn't the only reason she couldn't marry him. And she wasn't even sure it was entirely true, because she suspected she was already halfway in love with him. Despite everything. How else could she explain the bone-deep yearning that had gripped her as soon as she had stepped into the office, the needs and wants that went way beyond simple physical desire, or all the dreams she'd had with him as the star player, not just in the last week but also the last month? Or her immediate decision to have this child, which she could now see with complete clarity was not just because she wanted a baby but because this baby was his.

No, the real stumbling block to a marriage between them wasn't her feelings, it was his. His refusal to accept that love even existed.

But as she watched the stark expression on his face, and realised the effort it was taking him to be reasonable, not to simply repeat the demands he had made a week ago, the foolish bubble of hope pressed against her larynx.

Surely no one's emotions were ever set in stone, even those of a man like Raif—who had spent years protecting himself from weakness, because of the appalling way he had been treated by his own father.

If she was already half in love with him, didn't she owe it to herself and their child to at least give him a chance, give them both a chance to find a compromise?

'Well, yes,' she said. 'That's part of the reason.'

'Then perhaps you could love me if you got to know me better. And we could be married, is this not also correct?'

But it's not just about me loving you, Raif.

The qualification screamed inside her head, but she could see the flicker of wariness he was trying to hide. And she couldn't bring herself to challenge his interpretation of the obstacles to their marriage. Not yet.

This was a man who had never known love, had persuaded himself he didn't need it or want it. That it didn't even exist. At least not for him. And because of the terrible things he had confided in her, she knew why he felt that way. But still he was here willing to talk about it to her. Willing to take her needs seriously.

Yes, she would have a mountain to climb to persuade him he did need love in his life. And she didn't want to put herself in the position of trying to make him love her, because that way could only lead to heartache. She knew how painful and pointless such an endeavour was because she had blamed herself for her mother's absence. She had finally grown up enough to realise her love could never have been enough to make her mother stay—that she couldn't hold herself responsible for her mother's choices.

But what choice had Raif ever had to understand and embrace the importance of love if no one had ever loved him unconditionally? Perhaps he would never have the ability to do that with her, but she wanted so much for him to be able to find that with their child. Surely as long as she protected her own heart, there was nothing to be afraid of, or not much.

She let the bubble of hope expand in her throat. 'Perhaps,' she said.

'Then I have a suggestion,' he said.

Anticipation leapt under her breastbone.

'I have important business to attend to in Paris

and New York over the next three weeks,' he began as he planted his hands in his pockets and turned back towards the sunlight, breaking eye contact as he spoke. His devastatingly handsome profile made her heartbeat accelerate.

Not fair.

'Business I cannot ignore and that was neglected while I was recovering at the Golden Palace.' He mentioned his illness with pragmatism, making her sure he hadn't intended to make her feel guilty, but she felt the pang nonetheless. 'But there will be some free time between meetings when we can spend time together...' He turned, the desire in his eyes intensifying as his gaze fixed on her face, direct and dogmatic and as overwhelming as always.

She ought to be wary of his request. Spending three weeks with this man had the potential to seriously endanger her heart. But then his Adam's apple bobbed.

He was nervous, or at least apprehensive, about her answer and trying extremely hard not to show it.

It was the first time she'd ever been able to read him, the first time she'd seen a crack in the wall of confidence he presented to the world.

The bubble of hope swelled to the size of a hot-air balloon in her chest.

This was progress. Maybe it was only baby steps, but still it felt important and exhilarating in a way she would never have believed possible. And it felt like enough, for now.

'Will you come with me?' he asked, his tone curt. But the edge of uncertainty made the hot-air balloon bob under her breastbone.

'Yes,' she said, fighting her own fears to give them both a chance.

'Good.' He whipped his hands out of his pockets, cradled her cheeks between rough palms and captured her lips with his.

The kiss was deep, hungry and demanding. His tongue explored the recesses of her mouth, commanding her response—which rioted through her body on a wave of emotions she couldn't even begin to control.

But when they finally parted, the line of his jaw had softened, and along with the hunger, the satisfaction, the cast-iron confidence she could see the flicker of relief, and it was enough to steer the hot-air balloon full of hope towards her heart.

CHAPTER FOURTEEN

KASIA SIGHED AS she stepped onto the balcony of the Parisian hotel's penthouse suite. The Eiffel Tower seemed close enough to touch, its elegant steel beams lit by a million tiny lights in the sunset, while it watched over the warren of streets like a benevolent giant.

'Wow.' She spun round as Raif joined her on the terrace, having just tipped the battalion of porters who had brought up their luggage. 'This view is incredible.'

'I'm glad you approve.' He wrapped an arm around her waist to pull her back against his body. His lips found the rapidly beating pulse in her neck—the pulse that hadn't stopped fluttering since he'd arrived at her hall of residence in a chauffeur-driven car three hours ago. The pulse that had been going a little haywire ever since: when he'd escorted her aboard the Kholadi Corporation's private jet; when they'd been picked up by another chauffeur-driven car at Orly Airport; when he'd pointed out the cluster of iconic landmarks they'd passed on the drive through the Eighth Arrondissement to their hotel.

She had sighed over the elegance of the Élysée Palace, gawped at the splendour of the Grand Palais, fed her passion for people watching as they'd cruised down the Champs-Élysées and almost got a crick in her neck as they'd passed the Arc de Triomphe. She'd never been to Paris before, had never really been outside Cambridge during her five years in Europe, having been far too focused on her studies.

But her elevated pulse as she took in the magnificence of the City of Light for the first time had more to do with the man beside her and the thought of spending three whole weeks in his company.

She had made a decision the day before, after they had parted in Walmsley's office and he had contacted her later that day with details of their trip, that she would embrace the chance he was giving her to get to know him. He wanted this trip to end in marriage, she understood that. And she had no doubt at all that he would pull out all the stops to make that happen.

But just because he wanted marriage for all

the wrong reasons—for honour, and duty and responsibility and because she was carrying his child—it didn't mean they couldn't fall in love, or at least use this trip to find an accord that would stand them in good stead when they became parents.

She wasn't going to rule anything out. She wanted to keep her heart and her mind open, to absorb every sight and sound and sensation and to discover everything she could about a man who had always fascinated her.

Raif trailed kisses up her neck, the teasing licks and nips of his tongue and teeth sending the familiar shivers of anticipation darting down to her core. She softened against him, the magnificent view nowhere near as awesome as the feel of having his arms around her again. She tilted her head to give him better access, and covered his hands with hers as her breathing accelerated.

He hadn't touched her since the kiss they had shared to seal the deal they'd made in Walmsley's office. And she'd been looking forward to continuing their sexual relationship every moment since—because sex was the one thing in their relationship that was uncomplicated and straightforward. And sex seemed like the perfect way to get closer to him, to continue knocking down the wall he used to shut people out.

Feeling his erection pressing against her back, she shifted in his arms, more than ready to take his tantalising kisses to the next level. But as she lifted her arms to draw him closer, his hands gripped her waist, keeping her at arm's length.

'Stop, my little witch,' he said, a tight smile on his face. 'We cannot.'

'Why not?' she asked, unable to hide her disappointment as she let her arms drop, suddenly hesitant and unsure of herself.

'There is not enough time,' he said, as he brushed a thumb across her cheek, setting off all the usual reactions at her core. 'I have an important meeting to attend this evening.'

'Really?' she said, perplexed now as well as disappointed. 'But it's almost dark.' And she'd been looking forward to some quality time alone with him ever since yesterday's kiss.

Why had he started something he couldn't finish? Her gaze darted down to the thick ridge in his pants that suggested she hadn't read the situation entirely wrongly.

'In Paris, they conduct business at all hours,' he said, giving a strained chuckle. 'I must shower and change before I go. And you should rest,' he added. 'It has been a long, tiring journey.'

No, it hadn't. He'd only picked her up a few hours ago, and being transported in a chauffeur-driven limousine and a private jet—and waited on hand and foot—was hardly stressful.

'I'm not tired,' she said. Then, getting up all her courage, she added, 'Perhaps I could join you in the shower?'

His pupils dilated to black and his jaw tensed, but the tight smile remained as he shook his head. 'It is going to be a cold shower—if you join me, the purpose of it will be defeated.'

'Oh, I see,' she said, unable to deny the little leap of excitement that she could affect him in that way.

But when he lifted her hand to graze a perfunctory kiss across her knuckles, then left her standing on the balcony alone, the disappointment—and confusion—returned. Especially when she discovered Raif had directed the porters to put her two suitcases in a bedroom on the other side of the suite's luxury living area from his own.

Had she misconstrued his intentions? Should she say something? She had thought that they would be together. Really together. And it wasn't just about the sex, she wanted to share the intimacy of waking up in his arms, and discovering all his annoying little habits. They only had three weeks so why would he want to spend them in separate bedrooms?

'Will you be okay on your own tonight?'

She swung round from the balcony of her bedroom to find him standing at the door in a newly pressed suit, his damp hair slicked back, his jaw clean shaven.

She swallowed her disappointment and tried to contain the inevitable leap of lust. She was being ridiculous, this was their first night, he was giving her space, being considerate. She must not overreact.

'Yes, of course,' she said.

He strode towards her, and clasped her face in his hands. 'Order something from room service, there is a Michelin-starred chef here, I believe.'

'You won't be back in time for dinner?'

'I'm not sure,' he said, but she could see the lie in his eyes—she wouldn't see him again tonight. 'But if I am delayed, I don't want you to go hungry.' He gave her a chaste kiss on the forehead. 'Get a good night's sleep.'

After the main door of the suite had closed behind him, she turned back to the romantic view, which seemed to be mocking her. The sun had almost disappeared behind the rooftops, making the lights on the iconic tower glow orange in the dusk. She let out a tortured breath.

Maybe a cold shower wouldn't be a bad idea for her, too, before she examined the room service menu.

She had three whole weeks to get to know the father of her child, and she had this beautiful city to explore over the next few days while he was busy in his meetings. Intimacy couldn't be rushed. And they were as hungry for each other as they had ever been—a slight delay would only make them more eager.

She was being paranoid and insecure, because she had no experience of how to conduct an intimate relationship, any more than she suspected Raif did.

She placed a warm palm on the waistband of her jeans, which had already started to get a little tight, and smiled.

She needed to slow down and enjoy the moment, and stop wishing for more, when she already had so much.

CHAPTER FIFTEEN

YOU NEED TO stop messing about and seduce him—tonight.

Kasia smoothed shaky palms down the purple satin of the gown she had been fitted for that morning in an exclusive designer boutique just off the Champs-Élysées.

They'd been in Paris for four days now—and four nights—and despite two evening meals in the hotel's Michelin-starred rooftop restaurant, when their conversation had been stilted and polite, she'd barely seen Raif or spoken to him. Part of that had been her fault. Each morning, after surviving the now regular bout of morning sickness, she'd fallen back into bed exhausted and woken up hours later to find him gone.

But the nights she had spent alone, deposited back at the suite with a perfunctory kiss and an increasingly banal excuse, were entirely Raif's fault.

Why didn't he want to spend any quality time

with her? Why didn't he even want to sleep with her? She knew desire was not the problem, from the way she'd caught him looking at her on several occasions before he could mask it.

Keeping herself busy and trying not to dwell on the progress they weren't making hadn't been too hard. He'd left a car and driver at her disposal and given her a platinum credit card that she'd used to buy a suitable wardrobe for the charity ball they were attending tonight.

There had been so many places to explore, so many sights and sounds to excite and entertain her, but underneath the excitement had always been the disappointment she wasn't seeing any of them with him. She hadn't pressed him, though, on the time they spent apart. She knew he was busy, and the principal reason for him being in Paris was his business interests in Europe. She'd been impressed with how hard he worked, had even been a little bit astonished to discover he spoke fluent German, French and Italian.

On the one morning she'd managed to wake up before he'd left for the day she'd heard him conversing in all three languages during a conference call.

But tonight was going to be different. They

were attending a charity ball at the Petit Palais and she'd spent all day preparing her master plan—to finally turn the heated promise in his eyes into reality.

The gown's classic lines and sleek, simple cut hugged her curves and managed to look elegant despite accentuating her increasingly generous bosom. Having spent most of the afternoon since she'd returned from the dress fitting visiting the hotel's spa—being buffed and primped to within an inch of her life—and then the salon where her hair had been tamed and styled into an elaborate chignon, she finally felt like a queen, instead of a serving girl playing dress-up.

Tonight was the night.

She stepped into the suite's living area and spotted Raif adjusting the cuffs of his tuxedo as he stood on the suite's balcony.

The heat fired down to her core. She took a hitched breath as she absorbed the sight, making the bodice of the gown tighten like a corset. The suite's view of the Eiffel Tower was magnificent as always, but it was the man—dark and impossibly dashing in the designer tuxedo and white shirt—who took her breath away.

Clutching the jewelled evening bag that matched the gown, she cleared her throat.

His head lifted and his gaze roamed over her skin.

Walking towards her, his lips lifted in a strained smile. 'You look exquisite,' he murmured, lifting her fingers to his lips. 'I see you put the credit card to good use.'

'I only had to buy the shoes and the purse,' she said, pleased about the bargain she'd arranged. When he was working so hard to increase the Kholadi's investment profile in the West, what right did she have to spend his money on frivolous things? 'The boutique was happy to loan me the gown for the evening when I told them the event we were attending.'

His brow furrowed. 'Why did you do this? I do not wish you to wear borrowed clothing.'

'But it was very expensive, Raif. Thousands of euros. I would feel uncomfortable spending that amount of—'

'Thousands of euros is nothing,' he interrupted her. 'Kholadi Corporation made over fifteen million euros in an hour yesterday from our investments alone.'

She swallowed, suitably staggered by the

amount. She'd known he was wealthy, but she hadn't been prepared for how wealthy.

'I think I can afford to buy the mother of my child a gown,' he added, cupping her cheek, his eyes flaring again. But instead of being warmed by the heat, this time she felt a little overwhelmed, the compulsion to stand her ground somehow more pronounced.

'Yes, but it's not my money. Of course when the baby's born I'd be more than happy for you to pay any support you feel is—'

'Stop.' He ran his thumb over her lips. Then pulled a small velvet box out of the pocket of his tuxedo. 'We are not strangers, Kasia,' he said as her gaze became fixated on the box. Was that what she thought it was? And how was she supposed to react? Because the sudden blip of panic was swiftly followed by an equally disturbing swell of emotion.

'I want you to be much more than just the mother of my child.' He flicked open the box, tugged out an exquisite diamond-studded gold engagement ring and then dropped the box on the balcony table. 'Which is why I wish you to wear this.'

He lifted her trembling fingers and without waiting for her reply slid it onto her ring finger.

She stood stunned, emotion threatening to close off her air supply.

'But… I haven't agreed to marry you, Raif,' she said, feeling sad at the thought that they were no further along than they had been in Walmsley's office when she'd agreed to this trip. 'It's a beautiful ring, but I can't wear it.'

But when she went to drag the ring off, he clasped her fingers, preventing her.

'Wait, and hear me out,' he said, his thumbs stroking the backs of her hands in a gentle caress.

Forced to listen or start a wrestling match, she waited to see what he had to say, the ring heavy on her finger.

'An engagement ring is a symbol of intention, is it not?' he said, his eyes guarded but so intense she felt the burn right down to her soul.

'I suppose so,' she replied.

'I intend to marry you at the end of this trip, Kasia, and I want everyone to know it, which is why I wish you to wear my ring.' His gaze coasted over the gown she'd borrowed, making the exposed skin of her arms and cleavage burn.

'And why I wish you to purchase everything and anything you need with my money.'

The possessiveness in his tone was so compelling it made her feel scalded, but what he was talking about was still rights and responsibility and nothing more.

'But I haven't agreed to—'

'Shhh...' Tugging her close, he kissed her, his lips silencing hers, his tongue driving into her mouth until she was breathless. When he finally released her she was more than a little dazed.

'Wearing my ring does not take that choice away from you,' he said, the fierce determination on his face only stealing more of her breath. 'But I am a proud man, and until you have made your choice, while you are by my side I want everyone to know you—and your baby—are mine. Do you understand?'

Oddly, she did understand. This wasn't about taking her choices away from her, it was about him asserting his responsibilities to his child and her. And maybe she owed him this much, even if it was going to make it harder for her to make her choice. But then why should her choice be easy? He was right, a child was involved now. Not just her. So she nodded.

'You will wear the ring?' he said, finally asking instead of telling her.

And because he had, she nodded. 'Yes.' Her lips quirked in an unsteady smile. 'And thank you.'

'You are welcome.' Lifting her left hand, he kissed the ring, and the lump of emotion made it hard for her to breathe.

But it was only as he escorted her out of the hotel into the waiting limousine, a protective arm around her waist, that it occurred to her that wearing his ring didn't just make her feel as if she belonged to him. It made her feel owned.

CHAPTER SIXTEEN

HOW CAN I want her so much, all the time? Why can I not control it?

Raif's fingers firmed on Kasia's waist as she shifted away from him to talk to some minor royal, who had been flirting with his fiancée for the last twenty minutes. Kasia seemed oblivious to the young man's intentions, or that the bastard had conducted their conversation about her research into desert agriculture almost entirely at her cleavage. Her lush, beautiful bust pressed provocatively against the purple satin as she gesticulated to make a point about Narabia's need for greater yield and the research she was doing into how to achieve that.

Blood surged into his groin, and Raif tensed, annoyed all over again by the effect she had on him. He had tried to be considerate these last four days, had deliberately made himself scarce—especially at night. She'd been exhausted when he'd seen her in Walmsley's office, the bruised smudges under her eyes disturbing him. And each morning he could hear her retching violently as she had done on their morning together two weeks ago. He would have to bed her soon or risk exploding. But it was beginning to concern him, not just how little control he had over his own libido but also the toll the pregnancy seemed to be taking on her.

She was radiant tonight—and all the more intoxicating—but he did not want to hurt her, to over-tax her. However, the more he tried to give her space, the more difficult it became to control the hunger. At least he had managed to get her to wear his ring. But as his gaze caught the flicker of the diamond on her finger, he knew it was not enough.

He wanted to stake a legal claim. He needed to make her his wife.

'Your fiancée is extremely captivating, Mr Khan.'

Raif jerked his gaze from the valley of Kasia's breasts to find the renowned Swiss financier he had been chatting with observing him with a knowing, masculine smile.

Embarrassed heat scorched the back of Raif's neck.

The older man had caught him checking out

his own fiancée while they were supposed to be having a discussion on… What had they been discussing?

'And intelligent,' the man added, as Raif tried to recall what exactly they had been talking about before he had been distracted—again—like a callow teenage boy. 'She speaks very knowledgably about your region's agricultural challenges. She will make you an excellent wife. When is the wedding?'

Good question.

'Soon,' he said, the frustration he was trying—and failing—to control, by avoiding his fiancée, suddenly making it hard for him to breathe.

A waiter passed them with a tray full of colourful cocktails. He rarely drank alcohol, it wasn't part of his culture and he preferred never to dull his senses, but he grabbed a Bloody Mary and knocked it back in one go. The salty fragrant flavour soothed his dry throat, but did nothing to sooth the hunger and impatience smouldering in his gut.

This was madness. What was he doing dressed up in a monkey suit making small talk he couldn't even follow and letting some over-privileged fool leer at Kasia's breasts when all he really wanted to do was strip her out of that provocative dress and feel those full nipples swell against his tongue?

Avoidance was not the answer.

'Would you excuse me, Stefano?' he said, dismissing the financier as he tightened his grip on Kasia's waist and pressed his face into the sensitive skin under her earlobe.

'Kasia, let's return to the hotel,' he murmured, as he kissed her neck and inhaled the intoxicating scent of jasmine and spice. The heat rose up his torso, but he'd had enough of caring about how primitive or uncivilised he appeared by mauling her in a public place.

Appearances were overrated. And he was not a civilised man. Especially where this woman was concerned. So why was he trying so hard to pretend he was? She was beautiful, captivating and wildly attractive, not just her body but also her mind—he'd caught enough of her conversation with a variety of people to realise that. Stefano was right, she would make him an excellent wife and an excellent princess. So why was he waiting to seduce her?

Kasia shuddered, her amber eyes darkening with surprise and arousal. The young aristocrat finally detached his gaze from her cleavage to frown at Raif. The superior, vaguely disgusted expression told Raif all he needed to know about the whelp's opinion of his behaviour.

He sent the pampered fool the caustic smile he had used to unnerve his opponents before the many brutal bareknuckle fights he had been forced to win to gain leadership of the Kholadi over a decade ago.

Back off. She belongs to me.

The young man got the message and disappeared into the crowd.

Satisfaction stirred, feeding the heat and the hunger.

Maybe he had masked the feral teenager he'd once been in designer clothing, and learned how to survive and prosper in the world of high finance, but the instincts of that wild boy still existed inside him and he had no desire to tame them.

'Okay, Raif,' Kasia said, the edge of desire in her voice only adding to the pheromones now firing his blood. 'I'd like that.'

'Good.' Grasping her trembling fingers, the ring biting into his palm, he led her through the crowd of partygoers towards the domed entrance of the lavish Belle Époque ballroom.

His impatience heightened as they waited for the cloakroom attendant to find her stole and his coat. He slung the stole over his arm and wrapped his coat around Kasia's shoulders. He didn't need the garment himself, he was already burning up. His hunger surged when he caught a flash of something raw and needy in her eyes as he escorted her into the street and flagged down a cab along the wide boulevard. He couldn't wait for their car.

The cabbie weaved through the streets in the short drive to their hotel. He kept her fingers clasped in his, stroking her knuckles, trying to reassure her as much as himself. Despite appearances and the judgement of other, more pampered men, he wasn't an animal.

And he would be gentle if it killed him. He didn't want to endanger the babe or exhaust her. But he could not wait any longer.

'Is everything okay, Raif?' she whispered in the darkness, and while he could hear the tremble of uncertainty in her voice he could also hear the naked desire that she was making no effort to hide.

Pride surged. Despite her apprehension she

was here, with him, ready to meet his needs with needs of her own.

'It soon will be,' he said, devouring the sight of her, silhouetted against the glittering lights of the city, as the cabbie drew up outside the hotel.

But as he escorted her through the lobby, dragged her into the penthouse elevator, and waited for the damn thing to finally reach their suite, he felt the tight leash he had kept on his hunger start to fray.

As they stepped into the suite, she let go of his hand to shrug off the coat and lay it on the back of one of the couches, revealing the seductive dress, and the lush curves he could no longer wait to caress.

Kasia's thigh muscles loosened and pleasure ached at her core as Raif's arms wrapped around her and his hands caressed the smooth satin covering her abdomen. His lips nuzzled her neck and her breathing became ragged, her heartbeat hammering her ribs.

At last.

The ring had thrown her and so had his presence by her side during the glittering event. She'd assumed he would leave her as he had so often in the last four days to attend to his business commitments. But instead he'd remained beside her, his arm banded around her waist, never letting her stray far from his side.

But what should have felt suffocating had been exhilarating. Feeling owned also made her feel cherished, and important. He'd introduced her as his fiancée and had never let her out of his sight. But then something had changed suddenly. She'd felt his irritation at the attention she was getting from the royal she was talking to and had assumed it was because the young man's conversation was so inane.

But when Raif had whispered in her ear, she'd heard the note of possessiveness, the note of arrogance and desire—and instead of feeling outraged or appalled she'd felt elated.

The journey to the hotel had been agony, her anticipation reaching fever pitch.

His large hands cupped her breasts, his thumbs stroking her nipples through the dress until she was panting.

'I need you naked,' he growled, his breathing as ragged as her own.

'I know,' she said.

He turned her in his arms, found the tab of the

dress's zipper under her arm. The sibilant hiss echoed in the shadowy room, the only light coming from the lamps outside. The evening breeze brushed over her skin, but that wasn't what made her shiver as he stripped the dress off her.

Seconds later he removed her bra. Bending, he scooped the swollen flesh into the palm of his hand and captured the stiff peak in his teeth.

He flicked his tongue over the engorged nipple, making the blood flow painfully to her core. She sobbed, the sensations unbearably wonderful as pleasure rolled and crested.

He lifted his head, his eyes dark with arousal. 'Are they more sensitive?'

'Yes,' she said on a broken sob.

He chuckled, then captured her other breast and continued the torture, sucking and nipping her into a frenzy as his seeking fingers slipped into her panties.

The heel of his palm pressed against her vulva. She rolled her hips, desperate to increase the delicious pressure, then moaned as his fingers delved, brushing and circling the stiff nub of her clitoris, forcing her to dance to his tune.

The vicious orgasm crested, her body bucking against his touch—so firm, so sure, so right. She cried out as she shattered, grasping his shoulders to stop herself from falling into the abyss.

As the last of the orgasm waned, her knees weakened, but as she threatened to dissolve into a puddle of passion on the carpet, he scooped her limp body into his arms and strode into the master bedroom.

He placed her gently on the four-poster bed. She lay there, feeling dazed and disorientated, her body alive with afterglow, as he stripped.

Her gaze consumed the planes of muscle and sinew, the scarred and inked skin, the scatter of dark hair and the large, thick shaft of his erection.

He knelt on the bed, but instead of thrusting that swollen shaft deep inside her, he cupped her bottom, draped her legs over his shoulders and blew across the slick folds of her sex. Then, holding her open with his thumbs, he licked across her clitoris.

Her body bowed back, the shocking pleasure so raw she could hardly bear it as he laved the swollen flesh, tasting every part of her. He held her bottom, anchoring her to his mouth as he finally found the hard nub and suckled. She clutched his head, scraping her nails across his scalp. Crying, begging, the pleasure too raw, too intense as she tumbled over again.

'Please, Raif, I need you inside me,' she moaned, as the waves of orgasm finally ebbed a second time.

She felt empty, she needed to feel the thick length inside her, wanted to see him shatter the way he had made her shatter—not once but twice.

As he rose over her, she could see the strain on his face, his eyes wild and unfocused, as he gripped her thighs, angled her hips and notched the wide head of his erection at her entrance.

But instead of burying himself deep, thrusting hard and fast, to ease the emptiness, he edged inside her so slowly her heart began to race, her body clutching and clawing at him.

The ecstasy turned to agony as he teased her, easing in so gently she wanted to scream. She was so frantic for the hard thrust she thought she might die if he didn't do it soon. 'Please, Raif, I need all of you.'

'Shhh… I must be gentle,' he said, the elemental groan full of the same raw desperation.

'Why must you?' she asked, the yearning so

sharp, so primitive she could barely think, let alone speak. What was he waiting for?

'I don't want to hurt the babe.'

What?

The raw pledge came so far out of left field it took her a moment to understand what he was saying. His sweat-slicked body was as tortured as hers.

'You are so tight, and I am not a small man.'

'You won't hurt the baby, Raif,' she said, even as her heart pummelled her chest wall at the taut desperation to hold back, to take care of her and their child, even if it drove them both insane. 'It's only the size of a peanut.'

'Are you sure?' he groaned.

'Yes!' She clutched his face, forced his gaze to hers. 'Please give us what we both need.'

She saw the moment the cast-iron control finally snapped. He grasped her hips and thrust hard, sinking right up to the hilt.

The brutal orgasm slammed into her and she heard him shout out as he rocked out, pumped back hard and fast—once, twice—then crashed over that final barrier behind her.

But as the pleasure exploded in her nerve-endings, shimmering through her body, her heart expanded in her chest.

As she drifted into an exhausted sleep, with his arms holding her securely, and the rapid rhythm of his heartbeat slowing in her ear, her own heart seemed to burst in her chest, the bone-deep yearning no longer contained.

CHAPTER SEVENTEEN

KASIA WOKE THE next morning to find the bed empty, but before she could let her crushing disappointment overtake her, she was scrambling out of bed and rushing into Raif's bathroom.

Ten minutes later, she was brushing her teeth with a spare toothbrush, her stomach finally having settled again, and making plans.

She must not get disheartened. They had made huge strides last night. Not just with the sex—which had, of course, been spectacular—but also with the engagement. Maybe Raif was uncomfortable with the intimacy of waking up together, but she would move her luggage into his room today, without asking for his permission. And make a suggestion for their two weeks in New York.

Her spirits lifted considerably when she walked out of the bedroom in her robe, ready to start fetching her things, to find Raif seated at the breakfast table on the balcony, reading a news-paper.

He put the paper aside and stood as she ap-proached, his concerned frown making her heartbeat jump and jiggle—the memory of his words the night before, in the throes of passion, coming back full force.

'I don't want to hurt the babe.'

Was that why he had been avoiding sex? Not because of a fear of intimacy but because he was concerned about her health and the baby's? Why hadn't she considered the possibility before? This pregnancy had to be new and scary for him, too.

'Are you well enough to be out of bed?' he asked, his gaze searching her face as he assessed her condition.

'Yes, I'm fine,' she said, realising she had a lot more energy than usual after the morning bout of vomiting, and even the smell of his coffee had not unsettled her stomach.

Holding her elbow, he directed her to the chair opposite his and seated her. 'Are you sure? I do not wish you to tire yourself.'

She heard the unfamiliar note of uncertainty. 'Really, Raif, I'm well.'

'But the vomiting,' he said, as he sat opposite her, 'it is so severe.'

So he had heard her each morning. And worried about her. The thought made her heart go a little crazy.

'Are you sure our...?' He paused, and she saw the unfamiliar flush of colour darken his cheeks. 'Our activity last night has not made it worse?'

'Actually, I feel much stronger this morning—despite the nausea,' she said, finding his concern utterly adorable. 'Apparently multi-orgasmic sex is a cure for pregnancy fatigue—who knew?'

Her heart leapt at the slow smile that curved his lips and the sparkle of heat in his eyes.

'Then I suppose it is my job to make sure you are supplied with it,' he murmured.

His phone buzzed on the table, disturbing the moment. Picking it up, he frowned.

'Is everything okay?' she asked.

He nodded. 'Yes, but the series of meetings I am attending in New York have been moved forward. I will have to leave tonight.' He wiped his mouth with his napkin and placed it on the table, before getting up. 'If you would like to remain in Paris for the extra days, I can arrange it.'

'I would rather come with you,' she said, perplexed by his offer until she saw the fierce satisfaction in his gaze.

Good, they were still on the same page.

'I will have my staff make all the arrangements so you can join me on the company jet this evening.' Resting his hands on her shoulders, he leaned down to kiss her neck. 'I do not want you tiring yourself, is this understood?'

She nodded, her heartbeat galloping at the delightful domesticity of the moment. But as he shifted away from her, obviously ready to leave her for the rest of the day, she covered one of his hands with hers and swung round. 'Wait, Raif—can I make a suggestion?'

'Of course.'

'Could we…?' She swallowed, suddenly nervous. This really wasn't a big deal, but it meant a lot to her and she was scared he might refuse. 'Would it be okay if we stayed in an apartment while we're in New York instead of a luxury hotel?'

His brows lifted a fraction, and his forehead creased. He was obviously surprised and a little suspicious of the request.

She rushed to explain herself before he could

object. 'It's just that I'd like to be able to cook my own meals.'

And I want to cook for you.

She heard the plea inside her head but didn't say it, because it made her feel suddenly vulnerable and exposed. Last night had been important to her, and not just because of the sex. It had deepened the intimacy between them and made her realise she was already more than halfway in love with this man. But she needed to tread carefully now, to make him see how much they could have together.

They would be in New York for over two weeks. While she'd loved sightseeing in Paris, and being treated like a queen, she'd much rather spend the time in New York making a home with Raif, however temporary.

'But there is no need for you to cook,' he said, clearly confused by her request.

'I know, but I enjoy it. My grandmother taught me how and it always reminds me of her.'

Her grandmother had shown her how to use spices, to judge flavours and juggle tastes, to create her own unique recipes, because she had considered it an important life skill for any woman.

'How can you keep your husband satisfied if you cannot fill his stomach?'

At the time Kasia had found her grandmother's thinking about marriage antiquated and silly, but she'd still loved learning the intricacies of Narabian cuisine at her side. It was something they had shared, her grandmother's way of showing her she approved of her, and she loved her. Unlike her mother. And it was a skill Kasia wanted to share with Raif, because she suspected, for all his wealth and status, both in Kholadi and in the outside world, he had never been nurtured in the way that only a meal cooked with love could nurture a soul.

She wanted to give him that, because he had already given her so much—she didn't have money or status, but she did know how to conjure magic in a kitchen.

His frown remained, but then he shrugged, and relief flooded through her.

'Okay, I will have my assistant rearrange our accommodation.'

She wanted to suggest she find the apartment herself, because she had visions of finding somewhere cosy and comfortable and intimate, and not too lavish, but she decided not to press him.

The apartment wasn't important, it was what they could establish inside it—a new level of understanding, of intimacy and domesticity. Together.

An apartment represented a chance to make some semblance of a home with Raif—with no staff looking over their shoulders and cleaning up after them, and no restaurant or room service meals they hadn't created and cooked themselves. To just *be*, in their own space, together, however temporary, was more of a luxury to her than going on shopping sprees with his credit card, or seeing even the most amazing sights without him.

As Raif left, her heartbeat galloped into her throat. It was such a small thing, a small thing that Raif didn't understand the significance of, but that was okay, because it had huge significance to her.

Plus she'd never been to New York before.

The next two weeks would be an adventure, for both of them, that she could not wait to explore.

CHAPTER EIGHTEEN

'THAT SMELLS INCREDIBLE—what is it?'

Raif dumped his briefcase by the door and tugged at his tie. He was tired. The day of meetings with a Mexican retail consortium looking for investment had been conducted in both English and Spanish—a language he was not yet fluent in. But as he slipped off his shoes and walked into the loft apartment's generous open-plan living and dining space he spotted Kasia, her wild hair pushed back from her face by a colourful bandana, busy stirring something on the five-ring stove.

His heart did a giddy two-step. And the fatigue lifted, to be replaced by the familiar punch of lust. And longing.

She sent him a quick grin, making the longing wrap around his heart. And begin to choke him. It had become a familiar sight since they had arrived in New York a week ago and his assistant had found them this apartment.

Kasia's request had confused him when she had made it in Paris. He always stayed at the Plaza when he was in New York. Had never had any desire to stay anywhere else. And if truth be told, he hadn't been that happy about agreeing to this shift. He didn't like her having to cook for them. And he liked even the less the daily excursions she made to scour the local markets to find the spices and ingredients she needed for her latest creation. But he'd had to stifle his objections because it made her so happy.

And he liked to see her happy.

Plus, the food she managed to conjure up— an eclectic mix of Middle Eastern, African and other ethnic flavours from her travels around the local neighbourhood shops—was quite simply the best he'd ever tasted. So much so he'd managed to regain nearly all the weight he'd lost while lying flat on his back at the Golden Palace.

'Sarma, moutabal and hummus to start,' she announced proudly. 'Then lamb tagine, whipped garlic mash and Armenian salad. I hope you're starving. The bread is from an amazing Lebanese bakery I found in Tribeca.'

After popping the pitta breads in the toaster,

she produced a tray of colourful dishes from the fridge.

'Please tell me you didn't walk all the way to Tribeca.' He'd cautioned her before about not taking the car and driver.

'Then I won't tell you,' she said, the flirtatious wink making it hard for him to be annoyed with her. Even though she had been defying his express order.

Dammit.

'Kasia, you must not tire yourself,' he said, trying to be firm. The nausea still hit every morning like clockwork. And he knew how tired she became in the afternoons, because he'd come back between meetings only yesterday, hoping to surprise her, and had found her fast asleep. 'Especially not cooking for me.'

'But I *like* cooking for you,' she said, disarming him all over again. 'Tribeca is not that far. And I had a nap this afternoon. So I'm not tired. Plus, the bread is amazing.' She pointed to a delicious-looking concoction, made with char-grilled eggplant, on the tray of dishes, attempting to distract him. 'And it goes perfectly with the moutabal. A lovely Lebanese man at the farmers' market on Hudson told me how to make it.'

'I don't want you talking to strange men either,' he said, frowning, as she whisked the pitta out of the toaster, chopped them up with a few efficient strokes of a very large knife and sprinkled them with some aromatic spice.

'He was ninety if he was a day, Raif.' Her eyes flashed with the rebellious spirit he had become captivated by. Taking the dish off the tray, she presented it to him with the plate of prepared bread. 'Now, stop talking nonsense and taste it, so you can tell me what you think.'

It wasn't nonsense, he thought grumpily, but then he tasted the dish. The flavours exploded on his tongue, lemon and sesame and garlic perfectly combined with the savoury charcoal flavour of the charred aubergine. A moan came out before he could stop it.

'Good?' she said, the eager smile making his heartbeat thicken.

'Excellent,' he was forced to admit.

'Sit down and sample the other dishes while I finish the mash.'

He did as he was told, perching on the stool on the other side of the bar as he had become accustomed to doing for the past week. He would ask her about her latest research, and the progress of her PhD, which the Kholadi Corporation was helping to fund after setting up the scholarship programme at Devereaux College. She would often ask him about his work, what he had been doing, and tell him what else she'd done during her day—which usually involved making friends with people she didn't know. And walking miles after he had told her not to.

But it was hard to chastise her when she enjoyed it so much. Kasia, he had discovered, was a naturally sociable person, who thrived on meeting new people and exploring new places.

Her stories enchanted him. And disturbed him.

How could anyone be so trusting? So devoid of cynicism? The question had begun to haunt him and make him feel vaguely guilty. After all, he was planning to use her gullibility—her naivety—against her to get her to agree to their marriage.

She launched into a story about the Lebanese man she'd met at the farmers' market. Usually he loved listening to what she had been doing all day, because she was an entertaining storyteller, and he found himself fascinated by how open she was. It also gave him no small amount of pride, her instinctive abilities in social situations, yet more evidence of what an excellent princess she would make for the Kholadi people. She had a genuine openness and honesty and seemed to be able to fit in anywhere. People gravitated towards her naturally—even he was not immune.

But as she talked about the Lebanese great-grandfather and how he had reminded her of her own grandmother, while she was mashing the potatoes, and he tucked into the delicious tray of *hors d'oeuvres*, the question that had been sitting on the tip of his tongue for days popped out of his mouth.

'Kasia, how did you lose your parents?'

She stopped mashing abruptly and lifted her gaze. A shadow crossed her face, and he wished he could take the question back.

'I didn't lose them exactly.' A resigned smile curved her lips, intensifying his desire to take the sadness out of her eyes. 'They lost me.'

He knew he should not pursue this line of questioning, he couldn't afford to get too invested in Kasia's past because it had the potential to make him even more conflicted about using her artlessness against her to get what he wanted. For himself, for their child, for his country. But he couldn't seem to stop himself from asking the obvious next question.

'How did they lose you?'

Kasia's heart lifted into her throat at Raif's troubled expression. He'd never asked her about her past before. She could see he was uncomfortable about asking her now. But the fact he wanted to know more about her seemed like another huge step forward, adding to the progress they'd already made since arriving in New York. The apartment his assistant had rented in Gramercy was, of course, a lot grander than what she would have preferred—with four bedrooms, a roof garden and the sort of stark, modern style that wouldn't look out of place in a design magazine. But the kitchen was magnificent and it hadn't taken her long to turn the apartment into a home.

Even though it had only been a week, they'd already slipped into a routine, a routine that involved not just spectacular sex every evening but also private dinners during which Raif devoured her food and discussed his work while taking a genuine interest in hers. But he'd shied away from more intimate conversations—until now.

As happy as it made her to have him ask, it

was also hard for her to revisit that time of her life. But she forced herself not to hold back. They needed to be able to share the truth about who they were and where they had come from. She knew the terrible degradation he'd suffered as a child, so why should she feel inhibited about talking about her own childhood?

'Well...' She concentrated on mashing the potatoes, not wanting to see his reaction. 'I never knew who my father was. My mother went with a group of other girls to the mining camps in Kallah to work and came back pregnant, she said by a French mine-worker.'

'So you are also illegitimate?' Raif murmured.

'Yes.' Panic twisted in her gut, which made no sense. Why would she be concerned about his reaction to her heritage when she hadn't agreed to marry him yet? 'Is that a problem?'

'How do you mean?' he asked.

'Maybe you don't want a bastard for your princess?' she said, forcing herself to voice her fears.

His brows launched up his forehead but then he laughed. 'The Kholadi have a bastard for their Chief. Do you take me for a hypocrite?'

She smiled, feeling stupidly shy under that intense gaze. 'No, I don't.'

He picked up a piece of pitta and dipped it into the moutabal, then directed her to continue. 'When did your mother die?'

She shook her head. This bit was tougher. 'She didn't die. As far as I know, she's still living, but she decided when I was four that she could no longer live with the shame of being the mother of a bastard. So she left me with my grandmother and never returned.'

He stared at her for the longest time, swallowing the food, then swore softly in Kholadi. Lifting his thumb, he traced it down the side of her face. The caress was light but very sensual, and the approval—and anger—in his eyes so vivid she felt as if he was stroking her heart. 'Your mother was a fool.'

She'd spent her whole life convincing herself she didn't need anyone else's validation, that her mother's choices were not her own, but why, then, did his support mean so much? She blinked, releasing the tears stinging her eyes. They rolled down her cheeks unchecked as a fear she hadn't even realised she had been holding inside her—that she might be as fickle and flawed as her own mother when it came to having a child—was defeated by the honest approval in his eyes.

'I am sorry. I have made you cry,' he said. But as he went to remove his thumb, she pressed her palm over his hand, holding it in place, and leaned into the caress.

'Don't be sorry,' she said. 'They're not sad tears.'

His lips lifted in a rueful smile. 'I am glad.'

Fierce joy pierced her heart—for all his wildness, for all his arrogance and over-protectiveness, the father of her child was a good man.

'I wish to make love to you,' he said. 'Will the food wait?'

Her heart jumped at the intensity in his eyes and she nodded. The mashed potatoes would taste terrible cold, but she didn't care as he switched off the oven and lifted her into his arms.

As he carried her into their bedroom and stripped them both naked, she tried to persuade herself it was the pregnancy hormones making her feel so emotional. But as he made slow, sensual, tender love to her, bringing her to an earth-shattering climax with his tongue, before thrusting deep and rocking them both towards another orgasm, she clung to his shoulders, trying to hold the emotion in, to justify and control it.

But as he worked that spot inside her that he knew would make her shatter, the pleasure slammed into her… And as her body plunged over that high, wide ledge, for better or worse, her heart followed.

Much later, as they sat in bed together, he fed her the cold tagine with his fingers, then licked away the juices from her chin.

She giggled, her heart lighter than it had been for a long time.

But then he cradled her cheek and her spirits sobered. His eyes had lost the boyish twinkle she had become so attached to in the past week.

'I must return to Kholadi in four days' time—the tribe is setting up a new encampment and I need to be there. For a month, maybe longer.'

She nodded, suddenly bereft that this blissful time together would have to end sooner than planned.

'I don't want to leave you behind. I wish to take you with me as my princess, Kasia.'

Her heart expanded even as her head cried it was still too soon for such a leap. She had no guarantee her feelings were returned, or would ever be returned, and her love for him was still so new.

But when he asked: 'Will you marry me?' she was powerless to resist the matching hope in his gaze.

She didn't want to be without him for a whole month. He was the father of her child. How could it be wrong to give their love this chance?

So she said the only thing she could. 'Yes, I will.'

CHAPTER NINETEEN

THE WHIRLWIND OF activity over the next few days was so overwhelming, Kasia had no time at all to revisit any fears she had about her decision to accept Raif's proposal.

They agreed her PhD would have to be put on hold until after the baby was born, but Raif was eager to fund additional research while they were in Kholadi as her work could be of great benefit to his people... *Their* people.

As he finished the last of his business in Manhattan, Kasia spent her time reading as much as she could about the Kholadi. She didn't want to be as ignorant as she had been about their lifestyle when she'd first spent the night with Raif. A licence was arranged at City Hall two days before their departure and they were married the next day on the roof terrace of the Gramercy apartment with his assistant and the building's supervisor, who Kasia had made friends with, in attendance as witnesses.

She made a tearful call to Cat that evening to confess all, and her friend had been thrilled at the news. Although she did chastise Kasia for keeping her affair with Raif a secret for so long.

'I cannot believe you're pregnant and married and I didn't even get to be maid of honour. You're also going to have some serious explaining to do to my daughter, who has been dreaming about being your bridesmaid since she was about two. And my husband, who would have wanted to give you away and have a completely inappropriate conversation with your new husband about his responsibilities!'

The memory of the conversation still made Kasia smile. How silly she had been to wait to tell Cat everything until after the marriage had taken place. Her wobble over whether Cat and Zane would give the marriage their blessing was even more ridiculous. They were her friends, so why wouldn't they be overjoyed for her?

Because they know he's not in love with you.

She pushed the niggling doubt aside.

That was her insecurity talking. Cat had only asked her if *she* was in love with *Raif*, so she hadn't had to lie. And maybe Raif wasn't in love with her *yet*. But less than a day after their marriage he was already giving a very good impression of an over-protective husband, insisting they stop off in London en route to Narabia to see a Harley Street specialist about her continuing nausea.

She'd tried to explain to him that it was perfectly normal to be sick and tired. In fact, it was practically a cliché, and she'd also pointed out there were a network of state-of-the-art maternity clinics in Narabia where she could get all the antenatal care she needed. But he had refused to be swayed.

So here she was, sitting in the elegant Georgian office of one of London's best obstetricians with her husband, having been whisked from Heathrow in a chauffeur-driven limo and given a series of blood tests by the practice's nurse.

'So, Mrs Khan...' Ms Siddiqui, the consultant, smiled at Kasia, her expression both kind and fiercely competent.

Mrs Khan.

'I've reviewed the notes sent from your GP in Cambridge and your blood tests. Everything looks good, although you are a little anaemic, so I would suggest we increase your iron. I understand from my conversation with your husband

that your morning sickness has been quite pronounced and you're often exhausted?'

Aware of Raif's eyes on her, Kasia replied, 'I'm
sure it's nothing out of the ordin—'

'Kasia, you are violently ill every morning—
surely this is not normal, Doctor?' Raif interrupted her, his concern palpable.

'Every pregnancy is different, Mr Khan,' the
obstetrician replied in a soothing but also firm
tone. Kasia's tension eased. While it was wonderful to have Raif worry about her, she really
didn't want him to worry quite so much. 'But
let's do an ultrasound to check everything and
put everyone's mind at rest,' she finished.

Excitement stirred in Kasia's blood as they
were led into the ultrasound room. Five minutes later she was lying on the bed, the cold jelly
smeared on her abdomen and the obstetrician
pressing the wand into the small baby bump.

The sound of a heartbeat beating in double
time echoed around the room as Kasia watched
the monitor, the indistinct shapes making her
blink back tears. This was her and Raif's child.
The lump in her throat grew and she gripped his
fingers. He squeezed back, instinctively answer-
ing her sudden need for reassurance.

'Aha,' Ms Siddiqui said, as if she'd just made an important discovery. 'I think we have the source of your nausea and the exhaustion, Mrs Khan.'

'Please call me Kasia,' she said as the obstetrician circled two of the shapes on the screen with a wand.

'You're carrying twins, Kasia,' Ms Siddiqui replied with a benevolent smile.

Twins?

'There are *two* babies?' Raif released her fingers, his voice raw.

'Yes, Mr Khan.' She pointed to the two shapes she'd circled. 'Here and here. And can you hear that slight echo on the heartbeat? That's because there are actually two heartbeats but they're beating almost in unison.' The obstetrician continued to press the wand into Kasia's belly, moving it around to get a better view of their babies.

Their *two* babies.

Kasia's stomach leapt and jiggled along with her heartbeat. She'd always wanted to be a mother and now she was going to be a mother twice over. She couldn't think of anything more wonderful.

But as the doctor took a series of measurements and answered all her eager questions about the pregnancy, Raif remained silent and tense.

Ms Siddiqui was fantastic, both pragmatic and kind, reassuring them that while the babies were big for the dates and a twin pregnancy was always more of a hormonal shock to the mother's system—which probably explained the nausea and the tiredness—Kasia was strong and healthy and once her body adjusted, everything should settle down. Raif did not look convinced.

'Are you okay, Raif?' Kasia asked, after he had helped her into the waiting car, as if she were a hundred and two years old and made of spun glass and might fracture into a thousand pieces at any minute.

He didn't reply to her question, his body language still painfully tense as he stared out of the car window at the passing scenery, lost in his thoughts. They were staying in a hotel in Cambridge tonight, so she could supervise the packing of her belongings in the morning, then leave for Narabia tomorrow evening to visit Cat and Zane and their children before heading into the desert and the Kholadi encampment in a few days' time.

She knew arrangements were already under

way for a royal wedding ceremony—their marriage wasn't legal in Kholadi, according to Raif, unless they said their vows in front of his people.

'Raif, is something wrong?' she repeated as the car turned onto Euston Road. 'You're not unhappy about it being twins, are you?'

He swung round, finally having heard her. 'No, of course not,' he said, but the muscle in his jaw was twitching so violently she was surprised he hadn't got lockjaw, and the expression in his eyes—hooded and wary—reminded her of the man she had first met in the desert. The man who had suffered a gunshot wound without saying a word.

He'd opened up so much in the last three weeks, she'd seen a softer, more relaxed side to his personality. And she'd loved meeting that man, getting to know him. But why did it suddenly feel as if that man had disappeared?

Stop freaking out. You're still suffering from mild shock yourself.

Two babies *was* a lot to contemplate.

'How are you?' he asked, his eyes narrowing as he studied her face.

'I'm fine. I'm great,' she said, wanting to reassure him, even if she was feeling a little weary.

And some of her own fears, about the burden of motherhood and how she was going to cope with bringing up two children instead of one, had resurfaced.

As excited as she was about this pregnancy, she also knew there would be struggles ahead. But she was determined to be positive. No matter what. One thing she knew for sure, nothing on earth would make her want to abandon these babies the way her own mother had abandoned her.

'Don't lie,' he said, reading her too easily. 'Come here.' Lifting his arm, he beckoned her towards him. 'Sit next to me,' he suggested. He unlocked her seatbelt and refastened her into the seat next to his. Then wrapped his arm around her.

She placed her head on his shoulder as directed, and listened to the comforting beat of his heart as her eyelids drooped.

'Get some sleep,' he murmured, placing a kiss on top of her hair.

She snuggled into his arms, the anxiety at his reaction—and her own irrational fears—fading as she drifted into an exhausted sleep.

They arrived in Cambridge at nightfall. After a light meal in the living room of their suite, he insisted on carrying her into the bedroom, undressing her and feeding her one of the iron tablets the obstetrician had prescribed.

She was so tired she could barely lift her arms, let alone persuade him to join her in their bed. But as he kissed her forehead, she thought she heard him whisper, 'Sorry.'

Don't be ridiculous, Kaz.

He was her husband now, the father of her babies. Both of them.

A weary smile lifted her lips as her eyelids shut.

Tomorrow they would travel together to Narabia. She couldn't wait to see Cat to tell her the news about the twins.

And then she would meet his people as his princess. What could her husband possibly have to be sorry for?

CHAPTER TWENTY

Dear Kasia

I have returned to Kholadi. I think the desert is not the best place for you, especially in your present condition, so I have arranged for a property to be purchased in Cambridge, where you will stay for the foreseeable future.

Internet connectivity is not good in the kingdom, but I will endeavour to contact you soon.

Dean Walmsley has been informed that your new research as well as the PhD will be fully funded by the Kholadi Grant to the faculty.

R

KASIA BIT HER lip so hard she could taste blood, desperately struggling to control the choking sobs lodged under her breastbone ever since

Raif's assistant had arrived five minutes ago to deliver his letter.

Not letter, she thought as she tapped Cat's name into her phone, Raif's instructions.

She had only just recovered from her regular bout of morning sickness and was eating some dry toast and wondering where Raif could possibly have disappeared to when the knock had come on the door of their suite. She hadn't even noticed that Raif's luggage and all his toiletries were gone until after she'd opened the cream envelope with her name written across it in his bold script and had read the devastating contents.

So businesslike, so polite, so unemotional.

Shock had come first. How could the man who had carried her to bed and undressed her so tenderly have written such a note? Had he been making plans even then to abandon her? He must have been.

Next had been all the furious questions. Why had he left her here? Why hadn't he spoken to her about his decision? Was she not entitled to a say in where or how she should live?

But beneath the questions was the devastating sense of déjà vu, propelling her back to a time in her life it had taken her many years to recover from. And all the fears she had kept so carefully at bay—on discovering her pregnancy, when agreeing to their hasty marriage, after realising she was having not one baby but two—leapt out of the darkness, too.

Suddenly she was that little girl again, small and defenceless, insignificant and unloved. That little girl who could never be enough, watching her mother leave without a backward glance as her grandmother squeezed her fingers.

'Do not fear, little one, your mother will return soon.'

But her mother hadn't returned. Kasia had waited and waited. And the only conclusion was that if her mother had ever loved her, she hadn't loved her enough.

The choking sob rose up her torso as the call connected.

Cat's voice came on the line—calm but concerned. 'Kasia, is everything okay?'

'I'm sorry I called so early,' Kasia said, the words scraping her throat as the sob pushed painfully against her larynx. It was before dawn in Narabia, she realised.

'Kasia, what's wrong? Has something happened?'

'He's left me. He doesn't want me, Cat. I knew he didn't love me, but I thought maybe…' The words spewed out, expelled on a wave of desperation, but were soon overrun by the choking sobs that racked her body in debilitating gut punches of anguish.

The crying came in waves, loud and raw and exhausting as she sank to the floor by the lavish four-poster bed and pressed her forehead to her knees, trying to hold in the pain, the devastation.

He's gone. He won't return. He's ashamed of me, as she was. Ashamed to have me meet his people. I did something wrong. But what did I do? How can I make it right? How can I be better so he'll love me? So he won't abandon me?

The questions that had tormented her endlessly as a child returned, like big black crows pecking at the scar tissue that had grown over the gaping wounds left by her mother's desertion.

She wrapped her arms around her knees and pressed the phone to her ear. But the choking sobs refused to stop, turning the anguish to agony.

'Shhh… Shhh… Kaz, you have to breathe… Try breathing.'

Her best friend's voice—soothing but firm—

pushed through the fog of devastation. Chasing the crows back as the heaving sobs finally turned to ragged panting.

At last exhaustion settled over her, she simply didn't have the strength to cry any more, her body wretched.

'Kaz, are you still there?' Cat said, a light in the darkness threatening to engulf her.

'Yes,' she said, her voice broken and raw but still there. She hadn't dropped off the abyss. That had to count for something.

'Now you need to tell me exactly what's happened,' Cat said. 'Can you do that?'

Kasia nodded. Then realised that Cat couldn't hear a nod, but as she gathered the strength to form an audible reply she heard a groggy voice in the background, asking what was wrong.

She'd woken up the Sheikh now, too. But before she had a chance to apologise she heard Cat's whispered reply to her husband.

'Your brother has been a monumental ass and upset Kasia. She's distraught. Next time I see him, I may have to shoot him myself.'

And then Zane's mumbled—and utterly dry—response. 'If he's hurt Kasia, perhaps she should do the honours. But tell her not to kill him, he's got a baby to support.'

Kasia dropped her head back onto the bed, the exchange between her two best friends making the strangest thing happen. A bubble of hope swelled under her breastbone. She placed her palm over the slight curve of her belly where her babies slept. Her and Raif's babies.

The devastation receded, to be replaced by something else flowing through her veins. Something it had taken her years to acquire the first time she'd been abandoned. Resilience.

The pain and anguish were still there. What Raif had done had been callous and cruel, he hadn't considered her feelings, hadn't even bothered to discuss his decision with her.

Her scars were rawer and fresher now than they had been. The fears real and vivid. But she wasn't a little girl any more, she was a grown woman, about to have two babies of her own. Curling up in a ball and letting these feelings defeat her wasn't an option any more. And oddly it was the knowledge that she could recover from this blow, because she had before, that gave her the strength to read out Raif's note to Cat.

Cat's assessment was stark and unequivocal.

'Kasia, that's ridiculous, he can't just decide these things for himself without even talking to you. In a marriage there has to be communication. I know you've only just fallen in love but—'

'He doesn't love me, Cat.' She forced the words out. However humiliating, however debilitating she had to own them, she realised. Because she had made mistakes, too. In her optimism and excitement about the pregnancy, about the man she'd discovered in the past weeks, she'd let her heart rule her head, had pushed all her fears under the carpet and married Raif without having any real commitment from him that he could ever love her back. 'And I'm not sure he ever will,' she added.

Her friend's sigh was audible. 'How do you know that?'

'Because he made it clear to me he doesn't believe in love—that he thinks it's nonsense. He...' She sighed. 'He had a miserable childhood, Cat. You know most of the details, I'm sure, from Zane. I knew...' She heaved a breath through her constricted lungs, the tears now for Raif as much as for herself. 'I knew it had hardened him, had made him cynical and determined never to trust anyone, but I thought...' She pressed her palm to her forehead, where a headache was starting to form. 'I still thought we had a chance, which is why I agreed to marry him, but if he doesn't want to share every part of his life with me, what real chance do we have…?'

'Okay, Kaz, listen, maybe I'm being the starry-eyed romantic now. But the note you read to me doesn't sound as definite as that. He's a guy and a prince, he likes to be in control, so he's making decisions for you both, but he doesn't necessarily know what the right decisions are. Did you tell him you love him?'

Kasia swallowed heavily, the rawness in her throat returning. 'No.'

She'd never spoken to him about her feelings or his. How could she accuse him of not communicating properly when she'd failed to do so herself?

'I thought that once we shared a life together, love would grow,' she continued, trying to explain the unexplainable to her friend. 'In New York and Paris, the time we spent together made me so happy and I think it made him happy, too. I fell in love with him but I didn't want to put pressure on him by making a declaration that might not be returned straight away…'

'I think maybe now is the time to put pressure on him. How can you know where you stand otherwise? And how can he?'

'I'm not sure I have the courage.' Kasia's heart thudded painfully against her ribs, that broken child coming out of hiding again. 'I don't want to risk another rejection. What if it breaks me?'

'It won't,' Cat said, with complete certainty. 'You're a strong woman, Kasia, much stronger than you think. You survived your mother's abandonment when you were just four years old. And let's face it, you can't possibly stay in Cambridge for goodness knows how long, waiting for him to deign to contact you. That's madness. You need to know where you stand. And he needs to stop acting like a dictatorial ass.'

Kasia felt a small, sad smile split her lips at the fierce determination in Cat's tone. Cat was such a good friend. Strong and supportive, always.

She wished she had Cat's confidence and her courage.

But then she rubbed her hand over her abdomen and imagined the babies growing there. She wanted to give them the start in life both she and Raif had lacked, of being cherished in the bosom of a loving relationship.

If there was a chance for that, didn't she owe it to her children to fight for it?

She would find the courage to go to Raif in the desert, where he had decided she didn't belong. She would defy his orders and tell him how she truly felt about him—and what she wanted in return. She would reach for the stars and if she fell short, if *they* fell short, at least she would know she had tried.

But whatever happened, she would survive, because she had to.

For her children, as well as for herself.

CHAPTER TWENTY-ONE

'CHIEF KHAN, an outrider has arrived from the Golden Palace—the Sheikh's party is coming.'

Raif straightened from his position—knee deep in mud—and threw down the shovel he had been using to dig a well with a group of his tribesmen.

The hard physical labour of setting up a new encampment had helped get him through the last few days. Ever since he had been forced to leave his wife sleeping in a hotel bed thousands of miles away.

The boy's shout in Kholadi confused him, though. What was Zane doing, coming for an official visit to the new encampment without informing him first?

They had been in brief contact a week ago when Zane had sent a text to congratulate him on his marriage. And Kasia's pregnancy. But that had been before their visit to the obstetrician in London. Before the fear for her safety had become so huge that Raif had struggled to contain it.

The shame had consumed him every day since, and the agony of loss, which he did not understand. How could you lose what you had never truly possessed? Kasia did not belong to him. She had married him out of duty, and kindness, would bear his children for him—and in return he had put her life in danger.

Was he really any different from his father? A man who had used women for his own pleasure and then discarded them?

Because of his hunger, his need, he had planted two babies inside her slim, fragile body. The doctor had said they were too big. He was a foot taller than her, it stood to reason his children would be too large.

He had killed his own mother, and now his children would kill theirs.

Rinsing his hair and chest in the bucket of water they kept next to the well, he picked up his shirt, annoyed at his brother's unannounced visit. He'd be damned if he'd get dressed in anything more formal when he had not been given prior warning. Zane would just have to see him as he was.

But as he picked up the dirty shirt to put it on, a thought occurred to him—and panic tore at his insides.

What possible reason could Zane have to come all this way—unless there was something wrong?

With Kasia.

Did Zane have news of his wife? Had something happened to her, or the children he had planted inside her? Had they killed her already?

Dropping the shirt, he ran, his heart thundering, his ribs aching with the pain that had gripped him for days—and the longing that tangled in his stomach like a snake and would not let him sleep.

He'd left her in Cambridge so she would be safe. But how could she ever be safe when he had put her life in such grave danger?

At last he reached the front of the encampment, just in time to see the pack of about twenty horses gallop over the ridge.

He spotted Zane at the front of the party, sitting easily on his horse, Pegasus, but next to him was a woman, dressed in traditional Narabian style to protect her from the sun.

Catherine, it had to be. Zane had brought his

queen with him. Kasia's best friend. To give him the terrible news.

His whole body began to shake as he sent up frantic prayers—to any god that might listen.

Please let her be safe. I will never touch her again, I swear.

The longing and the desperation seemed to tear at his soul as the horses approached, picking their way down the rocky dune. The female rider arrived first, her smaller horse stopping a few feet away. But then she tugged away the headdress masking her face and her wild hair appeared like a cloud of black silk.

Her darker skin registered. That exquisite shade that smelled of jasmine and spice. Not Catherine. Kasia. *His* wife. *His* woman.

The woman he dreamed about every night. Was he dreaming still? Hallucinating? Was she a ghost? How could she be here? He had left her in Cambridge, to protect her. How could she be in the desert? Riding a horse?

He stared, unable to move, the longing he had tried to dismiss, to live with washing through him on a wave of emotion so strong he could do nothing to stop it as his hungry gaze devoured her beautiful face, the guarded expression, the round amber eyes, the lush lips now pressed into a determined line. But behind the determination he could see the same longing, the same compassion that was making his own breathing ragged.

Was he going mad? Was this the penance he would have to pay? For his many sins against her? To see her one last time, with love in her eyes, and know it could never be real? That he didn't deserve it to be real?

'Kasia?' he whispered. 'Is it you?'

Her eyes widened. 'Yes, Raif, it's me. Now, could you help me down? It's been a long ride.'

The sound of her voice broke the spell holding him captive. And the longing, the yearning, the joy and the confusion suddenly crystallised into one unstoppable thought as he marched towards her and grasped her round the waist.

She rested her hands on his shoulders as he whisked her off the horse and cradled her against his naked chest.

'You are well? The babies are well?' he asked, the tremble of terror in his voice impossible to hide.

'Yes, Raif, I'm okay, just a little tired.'

She was real and solid, but he could barely comprehend the joy of that—or the inevitable tug of arousal that would never die—around the rising tide of his fury.

At his brother.

His wife had ridden for two days through the desert. Against his orders. Putting herself in grave danger. And his brother had allowed it. Had facilitated it.

He swung round with his wife in his arms to see Zane strolling towards him.

'Can you stand?' he asked Kasia, his voice vibrating with fury.

She nodded, her eyes wide with confusion. 'Yes.'

Putting her gently on her feet, he released her and marched to his brother.

'You son of a bitch,' he shouted in Kholadi, then heaved back his clenched fist and struck the Sheikh on the chin. The pain reverberated up his arm but he didn't care as he heard his brother's surprised grunt and watched him tumble backwards onto his rear end.

'You dare to put my wife's life in danger?' he said, in Narabian this time as he stood over him. 'She carries twin children.'

He heard the click of rifle firing mechanisms

engaging, and the shouts as Zane's men and his own drew their weapons.

'Stand down,' Zane shouted to his men, lifting his arm as he levered himself off the ground, rubbing his chin.

Fury still flowed through Raif's veins. Until Kasia's cry from behind him.

'Raif, stop! What are you doing?'

Her fingers gripped his bare arm, the jolt of awareness drawing him back from the edge. He turned and gathered her into his arms. He cradled her cheeks in his palms, then pressed his face into that wild hair, inhaling the spicy scent of her, letting the longing flow through his veins.

'Raif, you have to tell your men to lower their rifles,' she whispered.

He lifted his head, nodded to his men. Who put away their weapons.

Zane's hand touched his shoulder. 'I have a message from my wife,' he said, as he pressed his fingers to his torn lip, the slow smile on his face confusing Raif.

If there was anything amusing about this situation, he could not imagine what it was.

'I'm so sorry, Zane. I should never have involved you in all this,' Kasia said from beside him.

'It's okay, Kaz, we've always got your back,' his brother said, with a familiarity that had Raif's temper spiking again.

But the Sheikh hadn't taken his gaze off Raif, and what Raif saw in his brother's blue eyes wasn't the anger or contempt he expected but something that looked strangely like affection and understanding.

'What is this message?' he snapped at his brother, hating it that he didn't understand what was going on—not just with his wife and his brother but also within himself.

He'd almost started a war between their two nations by punching the Sheikh, but as he flexed his fingers, he knew he would do it all over again to protect Kasia from harm.

'Cat said stop being an ass,' he said, the smile that split his face only confusing Raif more. 'And talk to your wife.' Clicking his fingers over his head, he summoned his men to mount up. 'Now, I must leave you two if we are to get back to our camp before nightfall.'

'Wait!' Raif grasped his brother's arm, fury rising again to disguise his confusion. 'You can't leave Kasia here, it is not safe for her, she needs to return with you to the Golden Palace.' Perhaps she would refuse to return to Cambridge, but at least she would be well cared for at the palace.

Zane covered Raif's fingers with his and eased his grip, the look he sent him almost pitying.

'That's not my choice, brother, or yours. It's your wife's.' He glanced past Raif to the woman standing beside him and nodded. The silent communication between the two of them had the anger rising into Raif's throat even further. 'She's a grown woman, and your princess,' his brother added. 'She makes her own choices. And for some reason, the person she wants to be with is you.' Speaking to Kasia, he added, 'Kasia, I will wait at the overnight camp for a day. Send a rider if you would like me to return for you.'

He watched Kasia nod and thank his brother. He remained silent, so furious and confused now he could not speak. Then Zane bade them both farewell and mounted Pegasus. He waved once, then shouted to his men, urging the stallion into a gallop as he led the party back over the ridge.

'Raif, we must talk,' Kasia said, her voice quivering with emotion. But the unwavering gaze and the defiant tilt of her chin told a different story.

He scooped her up and began marching towards his tent, set apart from the others at the back of the camp.

'We *will* talk,' he said, struggling to contain his temper at this turn of events, and all the emotions that had been churning in his gut for days now, maybe even weeks. 'And then I will escort you back to Zafari and the Golden Palace myself.'

She could not stay here. Already his hunger for her was all but overwhelming him. He wanted her so much, but more than that he needed her.

He could not give in to that need. Because he could not risk destroying her, too, as he had once destroyed his mother.

'Raif, put me down, I can walk,' Kasia said, trying to sound firm and coherent.

Not easy when her emotions were in turmoil and had been from the moment she'd spotted him, standing strong and proud, his bare chest glistening with sweat, staring at her as if she were an apparition. She'd expected surprise, maybe shock, possibly irritation that she had defied his orders and come to the desert anyway, but what she had not been prepared for was the explosion of violence—and the raw emotions she had seen in his eyes. So much more than shock.

She'd seen the anguish in his face when he'd hit Zane and knew that there was much more going on here than she had realised.

'No,' he said. 'I will not put you down.' She clung to her husband's neck as he marched through the encampment, his people turning to stare at them both.

'Please, Raif.' She was squirming—his bare chest, the captivating scent of his sweat, the rough tattoo glistening on his skin, the scars she had become so accustomed to making her ache.

'Stop wriggling,' he said as he carried her into a large tent at the edge of a water hole. He shouted something in Kholadi to the older woman who was busy arranging his clothing. Kasia had been studying the language for over a week and followed the gist of it—there had been a mention of a doctor.

'Stop,' she said in Kholadi as the woman rushed to leave the tent and obey his orders, then formed a basic sentence, telling her the doctor was not needed.

'You speak Kholadi?' he said as the woman left and he finally placed her on her feet.

'I've been studying the language.'

He nodded, obviously surprised by this development, and she felt a prickle of annoyance. What had he expected? That she wouldn't bother to learn the language of his people? But before she could question his assumptions, the furrow on his forehead deepened. 'You must see the doctor,' he said. 'Then you must return to the Golden Palace.'

'I don't need to see a doctor. I'm perfectly fine. During the last week since I've seen you the nausea has started to ease, just as Ms Siddiqui said it probably would.'

'You have been riding all day in the desert heat, how can you possibly be fine?' His voice rose to match the fury she could see he was having great difficulty containing. But rather than be cowed by his temper, she felt strangely empowered by it. 'You should not have come here,' he added. 'Why did you risk everything?'

Kasia drew a ragged breath at the raw tone, the deep anguish in his words.

She'd travelled thousands of miles to have this confrontation. But this was not at all what she had expected. She had assumed Raif would be cold towards her, unemotional, dismissive. She had been prepared for the worst, that he would tell her he didn't love her, could never love her and then he would discard her—as her mother once had.

But he wasn't cold, or unemotional. His dark eyes flashed with more than temper.

It was something she had never seen in his eyes before, something she had not believed he was even capable of feeling. After all, he was so strong, so indomitable, so commanding, what could he have to fear?

The heat in her core flared and sparked as she took in his broad chest, the dark pants hanging loosely on his hips. He looked once again like the man she had first met, the Desert Prince, but now she knew that while this man could be wild and untamed, primitive in the best sense of the word, beneath that tough outer shell was a man who had cares and needs just as she did—who could be tender and gentle and kind.

Gathering the courage she had worked so hard to nurture all her life, she forced herself to tell him the truth she should have told him weeks ago.

'I came because I am your wife and I love you. And I want this to be a real marriage. If we are to be a couple, I want to share *every* part of your life with you, which includes living with you here in the desert, as well as living with you in Cambridge or New York or London, or anywhere else we need to be.'

He stepped back, the shock on his face as raw as the emotion. 'No, you cannot love me. I am not...' His voice drifted into silence.

She touched his arm. 'You're not what, Raif?' she said gently.

He gripped her arms and dragged her into his embrace, burying his face in her hair, his shallow breaths tortured as a shudder ran through his body.

'I am not a good man,' he said.

Emotion seized her own throat as she grasped his cheeks, forced his gaze to meet hers. 'What do you mean, Raif? Of course you are.'

'No, you do not understand,' he said, touching her cheek. 'I killed her and now I will kill you, too.'

Her? Who was he talking about? But as he continued, his voice breaking, suddenly she knew. He was talking about the mother he'd lost, the mother he'd never known, the mother he'd tried to honour by insisting on marriage all those months ago.

'I didn't pull out, I made you take my seed,'

he said. 'When you were untouched. And now you are bearing two babies. *Two* babies that are too big for you.'

Her heart shattered in her chest. The tears eased over her lids at the pain in his voice. The raw, unguarded fear. She had thought this man couldn't love her, couldn't love their children, when he already loved them—maybe too much.

'I don't want to lose you,' he said, his voice weary as she noticed the dark shadows under his eyes. How much had he slept in the last week? How could she not have seen how tormented he was? 'If you truly love me, you must go back and stay safe.'

'Shhh...' she whispered, the tears falling freely now as he clung to her. She stroked his cheeks, felt the delicious rub of stubble against her palms. And pressed her lips to his. 'It's okay, Raif. Look at me,' she commanded, and his tired gaze finally met hers. 'I'm not going to die. I promise. I'm strong and healthy. You have doctors here and midwives and there is a clinic only a day's ride away. Women have babies safely here all the time, even twins.'

'But they are Kholadi women,' he said. 'They are accustomed to the desert life.'

She smiled, impossibly touched by his stupidity.

'But I'm a Kholadi woman now, too.'

This wasn't about the desert culture, though, not really. Or her ability to handle the nomadic lifestyle that was so much a part of who he was. He knew that to be the Kholadi Princess she would have to embrace that lifestyle, too.

No, his fear for her life, was much more personal than that.

What he really feared was his own feelings, the way she had feared hers. She understood that now, even if he did not. Of course this was harder for him to navigate because she doubted whether he had ever cared for anyone the way he cared for her.

So she would have to show him how.

She took his hand and pressed his palm to the bump beneath her robe. She couldn't feel the babies moving yet, but the bump had become quite pronounced already.

'Do you feel that, Raif? Our babies grow inside me and I will keep them safe always. And love them the way I love you. Love is a gift and, yes, it's terrifying at times because you mean so much to me now that I couldn't bear to lose you either. But the only way we can navigate that fear is to do it together.'

He stared at her belly, his large palm resting on her bump. When his gaze finally lifted to hers she could read every emotion in it. Fear, still, and heat, but most of all love. Raw and basic and untamed. And all the more powerful for it.

'I didn't want to lose you,' he said. 'I wanted to keep you safe.'

'I *am* safe,' she said, with complete certainty. 'As long as I am with you.'

At last he nodded, then he dropped to his knees in front of her. Bracketing her hips with his hands, he held her tight and pressed his cheek to her belly. Worshipping her in a way she had never expected any man to worship her.

She threaded her fingers through the short hair on his scalp, felt his shiver of reaction and the leap of desire arrowed down to her core.

He lifted his head at last, to peer up at her. 'You refuse to go back?' he asked.

'Yes, Raif. I refuse to go back.'

Nodding, he got to his feet then lifted her into his arms and carried her towards the lavish bed at the back of the tent. 'Then I suppose I will have to make good use of you,' he said. And for the first time in what felt like for ever she laughed.

He made slow, careful love to her—too slow, too careful—as night fell over the desert, but as she reached one climax and then another and another, she felt herself soar into the stars, and knew that, however high she flew, her Desert Prince would never let her fall.

EPILOGUE

Nine months later

'CAN I HOLD one of the babies, too?'

Raif detached his gaze from his oldest daughter's wide dark eyes as she stared at him with complete and completely terrifying trust to find Zane's young son William tugging on his trouser leg. The toddler's eager expression had a shudder running through Raif.

No way, buddy.

'Perhaps when you are older,' he murmured, cradling his tiny baby a little tighter against his chest and rocking her gently.

The boy frowned. 'Why not now?' he demanded with the uncomplicated logic of a child. 'Auntie Kasia let Kaliah hold one, why can't I?'

'Because Jazmin and Amal are very precious to me. And I would not want you to drop them,' Raif replied bluntly, admiring the boy's audacity if nothing else. And deciding he would have to have another word with his wife. Seriously, was it safe to let a six-year-old with the temperament of a lion hold their daughters?

'But that's not fair!' His nephew pouted.

'I know,' Raif said, unable to hold in a rough chuckle as the boy stomped out of the ornate chamber they had been given for their stay in the Golden Palace, no doubt to tell tales to his father in the suite next door.

Good luck with that, buddy.

Zane would be on his side, because he was as protective of his children as Raif was of his. In truth, they had been having many surprisingly reassuring conversations in the months since the girls had been born—every time Raif freaked out over a bout of colic, or a sleepless night, like last night, when Jazmin had resolutely refused to settle. Every time Raif convinced himself he had to be the worst father in existence, Zane had been the one to reassure him.

'*Cut yourself some slack, Raif. And wait till they're six and want to ride a horse faster than you do before you freak out too much.*'

Raif let out another rough chuckle at the memory of that conversation. How times had changed in the space of a few months.

Strange to think he had found a friend as well as a brother while staying in the Golden Palace— waiting for his wife to recover from the excruciating twenty-two-hour labour that had brought his children into the world.

The terror of seeing his wife in such pain, and the responsibilities of parenthood had turned his old rivalry with his brother into something supportive and strong...rooted in the shared trauma of new fatherhood, no doubt.

It had been a steep learning curve.

Pressing his lips to Jazmin's downy soft skin, he inhaled the sweet scent, elated to see her eyes had finally closed. His heart expanded with love—and pride—as he returned his daughter to the adjoining bedroom.

His heart ricocheted into his throat as he spotted Kasia in the armchair beside their bed, nursing their younger daughter, Amal, at her breast, the bright morning sunshine gilding her skin.

She glanced up and smiled and his heart expanded another inch, all but gagging him.

God, how he loved this woman. Her smile, her sweetness, her support, her intelligence and her love.

He placed Jazmin in her crib as if she were

the most precious thing in the world. Because she was. She and her sister and her mother. If anything ever happened to any one of them, he would go out of his mind with—

He cut the thought off.

Do not go there or it will drive you insane.

He patted Jazmin's tiny back until she stopped struggling against her exhaustion and settled into a deeper sleep.

'Well done, Papa,' Kasia murmured around a jaw-breaking yawn. 'You finally got her to sleep.'

'Of course,' he said with a confidence he didn't feel, but was determined to fake as he straightened and walked towards his wife. 'One down, one to go.'

Kasia smiled a sleepy smile, her wild hair rioting around her head, the amber eyes, which he hoped both of their daughters would inherit glimmering with amusement. 'Actually, I think Amal has gone, too,' she said, glancing at the baby fast asleep on her breast. 'So that's one for Mum, too.'

Slipping one finger under their younger daughter's lips, Kasia detached the small cupid's-bow mouth from her nipple.

The familiar jolt of arousal shuddered through Raif at the sight of his wife's exposed breast.

He flinched, shame making him tense as he ruthlessly controlled the insistent shaft of heat, which had only become more insistent in the last few weeks.

What kind of a bastard was he that he could lust after his wife when she was nursing their child? And had spent so many agonising hours in labour a scant three months ago?

'Let me put Amal down,' he said, needing to do something with his hands. He averted his eyes from the display of soft, tempting flesh as he lifted his daughter from his wife's arms.

After rubbing Amal's back until she gave a satisfying belch, he laid her gently in the crib beside her sister's—amazed all over again at how small and defenceless his children were.

One day they would lead the Kholadi, because they were as smart and brave and strong as their mother—but as the pride rippled through him, so did the panic.

He forced his erratic heartbeat to slow down.

They were not ready to lead the Kholadi *yet*, or ride horses like his fearless niece Kaliah, thank goodness. He still had a few years at least before he had to worry about diplomatic incidents or broken necks.

'What time is it?' Kasia asked from behind him.

'Just after ten,' he said, keeping his eyes on his daughters until he could slow the blood flowing into his groin.

'Are you returning to the Kholadi camp today?' she asked.

'No, tomorrow,' he murmured, listening to the rustle of clothing. Was she undressing? The thought of her naked had a predictable effect, so he strode across the room to stare out of the window at his brother and sister-in-law's suite of rooms across the courtyard.

Lunch wouldn't be served for several hours. Perhaps he could interest his brother in a ride? Or maybe he would go alone. He needed to do something to take his mind off sex, and leave Kasia in peace to catch up on the sleep they'd both lost the night before.

'Wonderful,' she said. 'That gives us two whole hours to enjoy ourselves in the bath I had Ahmed draw for us.'

He swung round, shocked at the seductive tone of her voice. His eyebrows launched up his forehead, and his jaw went slack as a punch of lust hit him firmly in the crotch.

She stood virtually naked, her lush body covered only by a diaphanous robe. He could see the dark outline of her erect nipples through the fabric, the curls covering her sex. His shaft stiffened to iron.

'Kasia, what the hell are you doing?'

'Seducing my husband. What does it look like?' Kasia watched her husband's eyes darken with lust as power, excitement and passion surged through her.

'But you must sleep,' he said, his voice a croak of barely suppressed agony.

She knew how he felt. She had recovered from the twins' birth weeks ago, but he had not touched her since weeks before their birth.

She had acceded to his request that she have her children in the Golden Palace, instead of at their home on Kholadi land. She had even agreed—after much furious debate—to the compromise of staying in Zane and Cat's home until the twins were four months old, having finally managed to beat him down from six.

She wanted to return to her own home with

her children and her husband. But she understood how much the birth had taken out of him. He had been beside himself when she had been in labour, the fear in his eyes tangible. But she refused to avoid this issue any longer.

If she couldn't return home for another month, she could at least have their sex life back. She was the one who had given birth—not him—and the doctor had given her the all clear a couple of weeks ago. But Raif was scared to touch her. She'd tried to give him time, tried to understand. They were both tired, two beautiful but demanding baby girls didn't leave much time for them. But surely that was why they needed to seize every moment they could.

She wasn't tired now, she was hungry. For Raif.

She untied the robe Cat had lent her for this seduction, and let the silky see-through material glide off her shoulders.

His nostrils flared, his eyes narrowing and his breathing ragged. The pounding length in his pants became all the more pronounced.

Holding her shoulders back, she allowed him to look his fill.

Her body had changed. Her stomach wasn't as flat, her breasts not quite as firm, her hips more rounded—but the shyness deserted her as his eyes met hers, the hunger she could see in the chocolate depths as raw and potent as her own.

'What's the matter, Raif? Don't you like what you see?' she asked, bold and unashamed.

'You know I do,' he said, his voice husky with need.

The passion built, weakening her knees but not her resolve.

'Then perhaps you would like to join me in the bath,' she said, turning and walking into the adjoining bathing chamber, being sure to sway her hips to give him the best possible view of her backside. She heard him swear in Kholadi and smiled.

Petals floated on the steaming water that filled the bathing pool. She stepped into the fragrant warmth, loving the feel of the heat and essential oils softening her skin and easing the tension in her muscles.

She'd been planning this seduction for over a week.

She heard him enter the room, and channelling Salome as best she could, she scooped up some water and ran it over her breasts.

A string of curses was accompanied by the sound of clothing being removed in a hurry.

A loud splash was followed by callused but gentle hands clasping her arms and pulling her round to face him.

His huge erection butted her belly and she ground against it instinctively.

'You little witch, you know I cannot resist you,' he said—but she could see the shadow of shame in his eyes, as well as the desperation.

Cradling his hard, stubbled jaw, she pulled him towards her. 'Then don't.'

But before she could claim the kiss she ached for, he drew back.

'I don't want to hurt you.'

'The only way you could hurt me,' she said, taking pity on him, 'is to deny us what we both need.'

'Are you sure?' he said, his desire finally outstripping the panic and caution.

Gripping his broad shoulders, she launched herself into his arms, laughing as he caught her hips and she wrapped her legs around his waist. The head of his erection butted against the wet folds of her sex.

'Absolutely,' she said, as she sank down, taking him in to the hilt.

They groaned in unison.

The glorious feeling of having him back where she needed him spread through her like wildfire. Her heart floated into the cosmos at the thought of all they had achieved together... And the glorious journey still to come.

'Now make love to me like you mean it,' she said. 'Before our daughters wake up.'

He buried his face in her hair, pressed her back against the mosaic tiles of the bath and proceeded to work her eager flesh in sure, solid, overwhelming strokes.

For once, he was doing exactly what he was told.

* * * * *

LET'S TALK

Romance

For exclusive extracts, competitions
and special offers, find us online:

f facebook.com/millsandboon

⊙ @millsandboonuk

🐦 @millsandboon

Or get in touch on 0844 844 1351*

For all the latest titles coming soon,
visit millsandboon.co.uk/nextmonth

Want even more
ROMANCE?

Join our bookclub today!

'Mills & Boon books, the perfect way to escape for an hour or so.'

Miss W. Dyer

'Excellent service, promptly delivered and very good subscription choices.'

Miss A. Pearson

'You get fantastic special offers and the chance to get books before they hit the shops'

Mrs V. Hall

Visit millsandbook.co.uk/Bookclub and save on brand new books.

MILLS & BOON